Murder beside the Salish Sea

Jennifer Mueller

ISBN: 978-0692291153

DEDICATION

To the Pacific Northwest and Bellingham, WA
my new home hidden in the mist.

ACKNOWLEDGMENTS

Thank you to all those of Bellingham, that have given their knowledge, stories, and love of their home town in getting this book written. Hearing it sounded like Bellingham was the best compliment I could have been given.

While I tried to make this story as realistic and historically accurate as possible that only goes as far as the town itself. All characters and the Cherry Blossom Inn are unabashedly fictional, except Tim Kelti and you know who you are.

CAST OF CHARACTERS

Col. Brock Harker...............bomber pilot returning from European Theater
Tom Harker.....................................Brock's Father
Amy Harker (Amaya)....................................Brock's wife
BJ (Brock Jr.)....................................Brock's Son
Harry Kobayashi (Haru)...............Amy's Brother, a doctor Brock was in college with at one time
Captain Stephens.......Commander of Bellingham Airfield
Pvt. Kingfisher...Airfield Clerk
Mrs. Trevelyan...........An old friend of Brock's that lives down the coast at Chuckanut bay
Harold Campbell........neighbor that died while Brock was away, he owned what is now the Cherry Blossom Inn
Greg Hartman........high school friend of Brock's, lost his arm in the war

Cherry Blossom Inn Staff
Jane Briggs...The Inns owner
Mrs. Heinrichs.......the cook for the Cherry Blossom Inn and formerly for Mr. Campbell
Smitty...............Local Lummi man working as handiman

The Guests
Roy Carlson........................never says much about himself
Mr. Poole.........visiting his daughter and rather obnoxious
Lt. Kelti..............says he's with the Northwest Sea Frontier
Pvt. Charlotte Evers..Kelti's driver
Magda Starek.............................Czech femme fatale but is she all she says she is
Petya Ivanov................................Russian lend lease liaison
Pvt. Charles Greenly...............locally posted military man staying at the inn on leave
Daisy...claims to be Greenly's wife
Emily Vaughn...................................a guest that vanished

CHAPTER 1

The dreams started almost immediately in his exhaustion after 4 years of war. Years away, with the war on, it might as well have been a lifetime. Deaths for a lifetime filled only weeks. Going home, suddenly there was a childhood toy in his mind; it felt like another had played with it instead of him. Images of summers long gone smiled back at him, and Brock felt like throwing the pictures against the wall, if only they were real. A half full bottle of whiskey last drunk by his father sat on a table by the sofa. The woosh of bombs ripping through the air heading to their target filled his ears, destroying the world he once knew.

"We're coming close sir, you want to take over to land?"

With a start Brock woke to the wind coming off the bay, rattling the windows, water streaming down the curved glass of the B-17. The dreams came to him awake as much as at night. A world he had bombed into destruction, dark nights blacked out from retaliation only brought to his shattered calm that there was nothing left. Life as he knew it was gone. The clouds, turbulent and grey, gave some peace though. It made a poor day for bombing. The sea below him ran into the Cascade Mountains with an impressive show. Islands fell like gems from a necklace into the bay. Hundreds of them from rocks to massive land masses filled his view. 20 miles from Canada and

1

right on the Ocean. Well, the straits that led out to the ocean. The straits of Juan de Fuca, Georgia, and Puget Sound all ran around Vancouver Island out to the Pacific. Bellingham Bay was directly below. Banking the plane, Brock approached the airfield on the north edge of Bellingham, Washington, and he was home.

Climbing out of the cockpit, the silence was shattered.

"Colonel Harker, welcome to Bellingham airfield. I'm Captain Stephens. I have your quarters prepared. I don't know quite what to do, a colonel serving under me, never happened before. If they had said a guest I'd understand, but..." Stephens just kept going. "I've been hoping since I received word you were coming if you'd give the men here some lessons, they're all just out of school pilots that are getting hours. I know they'll be pulled out soon and sent to combat. We can't get a better instructor, 7 months with the Flying Tigers, 85 missions with the 8th Air Force over Europe. Pardon my asking but why on earth would they send a fighting ace up in a bomber?"

Brock let out a sigh; he just wanted silence. "Because, unlike most recruits, I could actually fly a plane when I joined up. My father was a pilot in WW1 with the Lafayette Flying Corps, already had me when he went over and my mother chucked him out for a myriad of offenses he supposedly committed. I could dog fight when I was 10. Only thing the man ever did for me."

"Supposed offenses, sir?"

Brock just frowned. "She wanted a divorce, but no one does that. So she said why not join up and fly, since that's all he seemed to want to do. Surprised everyone by surviving and she was stuck with him."

"And the Flying Tigers? Is it true you have the Order of the Cloud and Banner from the Chinese?"

He just wanted to go to sleep and not dream. "Couldn't pass up the money they were offering."

Stephens should have been in films, a character actor sort. You knew who he was the minute he walked on stage; he was the good to a fault guy that was seeing the heroine before she met the film's star and she dumped him. "No I suppose not. What about after?"

"I was trained as a bomber by the Air Corps. That's what they put me back into. When the Tiger program was closed down in '42, I arrived back just in time to head to England and do a few runs before they loaned us out to the 12th in North Africa. Then Doolittle took me back last year when he reorganized. We've stopped operations over Germany. They were delivering food to the Netherlands as I took off. It's a ground fight now. All up to how long it takes to capture Berlin." The Russians that had been taking Berlin were making good progress, but the snippets of information getting out weren't good. Raping, stealing, killing people that might have had nothing to do with the fighting. There was ending the war, and there was just terror. After the word of concentration camps being found and their horrors, though, it was hard to show much mercy. Still he could hope there was humanity left, hard as it was to imagine after 7 years of the world tearing itself apart.

Stephens opened the door, letting him into the offices. "I'm sure we'll benefit from your experience." He poured him a cup of coffee.

"I'm on leave. If you need a plane ferried, tell me, but give me a couple weeks before you plan any training if it's not required. I haven't slept well in weeks."

"Yes, of course. Have you heard anything about Japan?"

Brock could only shake his head. His wife's own family wanted to kill whoever came to stop them from killing whoever got in their way. People she'd never met, never knew. They gave her blood and America gave her everything else. "Just that it will be a bloody mess. It could be years longer."

"Kingfisher!" Stephens called and a man appeared quickly. "Can you show the Colonel to his quarters?"

"Yes sir."

"I don't suppose I could borrow a car," Brock asked.

Stephens narrowed his eyes. "They dissuade use of vehicles for sightseeing. Gas rations."

"If you had read his file, sir, you'd have seen he is from here. They have a house down on Chuckanut Bay," Kingfisher answered.

"Really?"

He just wanted sleep. "That's why I requested here. I haven't been back since before the war started—as you know, I was in China when Pearl Harbor was attacked."

Stephens waved him away. "Yes, have Sullivan drive him. I can't let you have the car overnight, but we can get you out there at least."

"Thank you."

Out in the office, Kingfisher looked up at him from his desk. He was Indian of some sort, not local; he knew enough Salish to recognize them. "Are you staying there your whole leave?"

"You might want to keep the room open for me. I was thrown out, and I don't know if I will be again."

"Yes sir. It's there if you need it. If you're gone from base though I would need to get you some ration coupons, or it will be a rather lean leave."

"It wouldn't be the first time I've thrown a crab pot to survive; how about we see how I fare with the old man first. I might be back on the first bus I can catch at this point."

Kingfisher just let out a knowing grin. "Yes, sir. Over a woman was it?"

He should have been dead so many times. Six times wounded, while men nearby died or were maimed. But the wound that hurt most was Amy vanishing. Half Japanese women had to watch themselves; she'd lived inside the exclusion zone, even going to college there. Amy, the smiling face from a life that was gone. Life that was going to plan until Pearl Harbor happened. China to Europe as fast as they could get him there, he'd never even had a chance to stop and find out what happened to her. Her letters just stopped, the letters he sent unanswered. His father hadn't approved and threw him out. That was the money he couldn't pass up in China, money to support a wife. "Isn't it always?"

When her brother came to stay summers during college, Tom Harker hadn't cared, but the minute Brock and Amy got close, all hell had broken loose. Amaya Kobayashi was not for marrying. His father was a racist sod that didn't like her blood alone; the woman took after her mother, and it was hard to tell she was half Japanese. As American as anyone whose family

4

had been in the country for centuries. It wasn't just Tom hating Amy. Bigot or not, he was a hateful man. Brock's mother and father had hardly talked while being in the same house. It wasn't a joke that she had championed him joining up for WW1, hoping he wouldn't come back. A volunteer even before the Americans joined the fight. A weak heart never should have killed her; she was far too strong a character. She was gone before he ever met Harry, let alone Amy. Now Brock had thousands in the bank and nothing more; he couldn't find the one person he loved, that loved him. The only link to finding out if she chucked him over or was in a camp with all the rest or even dead was a bloody old man that hated him.

ii.

Huge shipyards he didn't remember stood on the waterfront. The San Juan Islands lay beyond the activity, dark grey in the mist. The ones he could actually make out at least, each one a different shade as it filtered in the distance. Lummi was closest, almost black. There was always boat building, but the war had changed that to big business. The canneries hadn't changed at least, filled with salmon and vegetables from farms that filled the plains to the north and south. In an hour he could be in the mountains; they were thick with snow even in April. Mount Baker loomed on the horizon when it was clear. He'd not seen a sign of the mountain landing though. Too many clouds.

Standing at the Economy Food Store, he was at a loss frankly. People were everywhere, not one he knew. He didn't have directions for ration coupons, if Kingfisher had given him some at all. No points for a can of soup, but 30 for a can of peaches. Why that made a difference he didn't know.

"Excuse me Ma'am, but..."

She turned quickly. "Brock, it can't be."

He didn't expect to find an old woman he knew. Rationing hadn't done anything to her wardrobe, but then she was wearing the same thing she did when he last saw her. Her husband was a big yachtsman in his day; she still dressed for sailing. "Dear lord, Mrs. Trevelyan. I didn't expect to see you."

She hugged him tight. "Then you're on leave, you look whole."

"I'm on detached service to the air field here. A fancy way of saying I have to work while I rest. Got some Captain feeling superior because he has a Colonel under his control. Figured if they were sending me it might as well be at home." It was the only place he could think of looking for Amy, frankly. It would be close enough to take a bus down to Seattle and her family. Assuming they were there to find.

"You need help getting out to the house then?"

"No I have a car waiting. I thought I'd pick up things since I know I'm not welcome. Somebody might have told me shopping is hopeless though. Flying a B-17 seems to have fewer rules."

"Don't you have a ration card?"

"I haven't been a civilian since 1939."

"What was it the papers said, 80 missions? Well you certainly can fly planes; there's no denying that. Known that since you were an insolent boy wanting to take my granddaughter to the dance, and you already knew how then."

Brock's smile faded. That seemed a lifetime ago now. "How is Susan?"

The woman's eyes softened. "She has two young ones to keep her busy, and building ships for good pay down at Bremerton. Her husband works at the same place." Mrs. Trevelyan leaned next to him close so no one heard. "Go see Mrs. Heinrichs and give her a wink. She'll set you up. Always has extra and I noticed on my watch duties that she had a new delivery not long ago."

"Is she still there? Mr. Campbell died, I heard just after I left for China."

"Oh it has a new owner, she stayed on."

"What watch duties are you talking about?"

"There's a defense post by my house, all those of us on the bay take our turn watching for the enemy. So far we've only had false alarms, but we always watch. They have big guns stationed out there as well, just in case. I'll have to tell Susan I saw you, but right now I'm late, dear." She was gone before he had a chance to say anything more.

He kept his eyes ahead as the airman drove him south out of town on alternate 99. More colorfully known as liquor runners' road. He should know. A man in the store had helped him get a few things that weren't rationed at least, but it wasn't much. The clouds playing over the islands and the coast had more drama to them than any clear sky. Mist rolled in off the water and weaved through the trees that stood along the narrow road on a steep hillside. There had been so much going on along that stretch once, brick factories, limestone quarries, logging, coal mining, even. But never quite enough people around to impede his father from making runs to Canada for whiskey; boats by the thousands could get lost in among the islands. Now black-tailed deer grazed on the early spring growth in the ruins of them. Blackberries would be thick once the season came. There were houses, and a few businesses. A cannery, a ferry to the islands, a chicken farm, the Chuckanut Shell, a rather good restaurant. Summers they'd taken the old sail boat out among the islands and crabbed, musseled, and fished their way around. Harry had loved it, Haru on his birth certificate. The next year he brought his sister. Years Brock looked forward to her coming, it was her sophomore year of University of Washington when he'd joined the Air Corps. He had graduated flying school before he came back on leave. Amy was there even if Harry was unable to get away; he was busy continuing school to be a doctor. They sailed out with his father scowling at them.

Anchored off Sucia Island an old haunt from Prohibition days, Amy had come up from the cabin in his robe. "Draw me, Brock," she whispered as she undid the tie.

"Amaya, you shouldn't do that."

"Why?"

"You know." She was going to kill him, that was why. A man couldn't get her out of his head. Beautiful, smart, playful, loyal, and more to the point he'd fallen in love with her. He'd drawn her for years already, first dressed and then moments when Harry was gone it turned far more erotic the older she

got. She was 17 the first summer, now she was half through with college herself.

She straddled his lap and smiled. It was the most beautiful smile he'd ever seen. "Yes, I know, and I should do exactly this. Draw me so you remember every inch when you've gone."

"I don't need a drawing to remember you. Every end of summer I loathe because it takes you away, and I spend the rest counting the days till you come back."

"Then make me your wife."

Dark sparkling orbs kept him from gaping. "You can't mean..."

"Yes, you big oaf. You think I'm sitting here in nothing but a man's robe offering him a proper goodbye..."

She couldn't say anything more; his mouth covered hers. "You love me? I spent the last couple years thinking..."

"I had to convince Harry he was busy just to come let you know since you seem to be as dense as oatmeal. The man's worse than an old woman at chaperoning. I refuse to let you go off to all those cathouses and desperate women off base and have your head turned. You're mine. You'll have to teach me though how to go through with all these naughty thoughts in my head."

"Teach you? You think I'm so...Harry told you about the visits to the brothels the summer before you came with us."

Amy rested her forehead on his. "He was bragging to his friends in the other room. Somehow I never saw the man that would do that when I met you finally."

"Father bought me a woman for my 16th birthday, and my 17th, and my 18th. Men need to know how to be a man, he calls it. Then Harry showed up and it was quite obvious he'd never so much as kissed a girl. So my father bought us both a woman. Why do you think my mother was annoyed at him years ago during the war? He wasn't buying a time for his son, he was a regular visitor—he doesn't know they told me they gave him mine for free, he came in so often even before mother found out. Bellingham was a rowdy town, and he was one of the rowdiest of the lot."

"And you just drew me without even getting the idea that I wanted you to come closer. You think I was just being a tease."

"Your father made it rather clear he was going to marry you off to a good proper husband, an all Japanese husband. The fact he hadn't done the same didn't matter, I guess."

Amy lifted her head. "But my father isn't the one telling you he can't live without you. Brock, I know I still have several years of school, but I can't think of anything else but you."

He didn't have to be told twice. "I'll marry you...after."

He woke from the first dream in months that wasn't of the world blowing apart as the car pulled to a stop. His grandparents had built the house when there was hardly a road, deep-red shingles on 2 stories and trimmed with cream and lots of sandstone stairs and pillars from the quarry just down the road. Madrona trees with their reddish bark, cedars and pines stood guard at least until the hard storms of winter battered at it. It sat on a cliff keeping it safe from heavy storm surge, the frontage facing the sea where no one saw it but passing boats. A porch wrapped around three sides, giving it unbeaten views of the islands, a balcony off the master bedroom the best of all. It fit there as much as any house he had seen.

He lived there because his parents had nothing, catching crabs and finding shellfish to stretch the bits they could earn among the 5 of them. Once there was money, but not now. Now there was just a house. His grandfather was a lawyer; he'd built a grand house there 50 years before. His father was a waster, all told. A disappointment to the big law man that had been judge and even in the state legislature. His father, Tom, schemed and scammed, expecting his father to clean up his mess. A pilot was honorable in war time, but during peace time it was a diversion, nothing more, and so when Prohibition came and a fortune could be made, he'd jumped at it. The house was paid for, they ate during the Depression with just enough left to send him to school. His grandfather left him money to go to college, geography and art aiming at map-making, where he met a young man named Haru. He was to be something he wasn't raised to be. After the lawyer died, things were rough and tumble with a waster at the head; his grandfather made sure he got out of there.

"If I was you I'd head to the Cherry Blossom Inn for dinner?" Sullivan announced. "That box doesn't look too filling."

"Where's that?"

"Oh right, things have changed since you left. Old Mr. Campbell's place, he died some years ago, and this woman named Jane Briggs bought it, must have been in '41. She's turned it into an inn now. It does quite the business for military men coming for vacations, take a bus right from Seattle there."

"This inn is next door, you mean? Has a Mrs. Heinrichs as the cook?"

"That's it."

Brock started laughing. "Then I know where I'm eating dinner."

"You know her then."

"Her Sahne Schnitzel, hmm."

"You want to know why I know so much about the place, it's the maid. She started a couple months ago, all us men come down when we get a night off just to stare. Other places for action, but for pure staring it's next door."

"Thank you for the ride."

His grandfather was a craftsman proponent when the money was there. An impressive inglenook surrounded the fireplace in the reception hall. High paneling, beamed ceilings, the house was gorgeous. It was a showpiece to a life that was a sham, and a half-filled bottle of whiskey still sat by the sofa like always. Left there just to annoy his mother even after she died years before. It was a time capsule, walking into the life he knew was gone. But not completely—the bathrooms had been redone, and the kitchen. The house didn't have electricity, phone, or indoor toilets when he last saw it. The water it used had been from a well. All the modern conveniences were there now, even a water heater. The question was how; his father refused to work. Fashionable navy blue and yellow filled the kitchen as he put down the box. "Father!" He braced himself for yelling, he was kicked out, but there was nowhere else to go.

Nothing but silence. Putting things up, the fridge had food in it, more than a man alone would need. Going back outside, the car was gone from the garage. The chicken coop was full though, and he grabbed some eggs to make. Brock poured himself a glass and found a chair overlooking the bay. The massive cedars gave their scent to the damp air. Even the water below the cliff stood silent. Not straight tall cliffs, they were odd stone sculptures battered smooth by the water and rocks, leaving holes dug out like ancient cave houses. The tide was in and a carpet of seaweed broken free of the seafloor was just below the trees leaning out over the water. An enormous bull whip it looked like, but was kelp caught on a rock. All the flotsam would be stranded on the beach when it went out again. Then a large stone beach would spread out before the house, a small stream running out into the bay through the rocks. A lone fishing boat slowly ran by, the only life on the water. Exhaustion took over; he slept at long last.

iiii.

Voices sounded odd in the midst of nothingness and his plane forever diving because there was no earth to crash into. He'd destroyed all there was. With a scream he woke up to find a boy staring at him, his father Tom came running to the door and almost fell over when he saw him.

"Oh damn." Thomas Harker muttered. "Oh damn. Oh damn."

"Are you all right, Tom?" a woman called. In the haze of dream and sleep it took a moment to realize it wasn't a stranger.

"Oh damn." Tom said again.

His memories of life came running quickly. Musk, sandalwood and amber filled the air, overpowering even the cedars, and Brock lifted his head. She was stunning. Exotic and all American, at the same time. Full lips begged to be kissed. Porcelain skin, dark wavy hair, and midnight eyes. The tears filled Amaya Kobayashi's eyes soon enough and she fell without grace on the floor. Sobbing filled the air. "They said you were dead." It was the only thing he made out of the noise over and over again.

The boy came running at him, hitting his leg with small fists. "Go away. You're hurting her."

Brock grabbed hold of his arms stopping the onslaught.

"That's your father," Amy said finally.

Brock froze. There was no doubt of it when he had a chance to look.

The boy stopped struggling to kick him with his hands out of commission. "You said he was dead."

"I thought he was."

"Will you not hit me?" Brock asked and the boy nodded. Slowly he let go and the boy just stared at him. "What's your name?"

"Brock. Mama calls me BJ for Brock Junior."

His eyes closed for a moment. He was not ready for this. Not unwelcome, but not ready either.

"Oh damn," his father still said.

"Can you say anything else besides that?" Brock snapped.

"What? Oh. I'm sorry, but..."

"It was getting annoying."

Finally Tom pulled it together. "What are you doing here?"

"They thought I needed leave at very long last, more than a weekend in London or Cairo." The sobs brought him back quickly though and he picked Amy up off the floor. She curled up against him as he sat again like she had so many times.

"I get that I left something behind, but it's been 4 years no one tried to tell me I had a son. You just dropped off the face of the earth."

It was his father that spoke though. "I didn't even have to ask when I looked at the boy, he's got your green eyes because you were fool enough to..."

"Fool enough to what? I married her in 1940. We just didn't tell anyone. All she had to do was finish her degree while I was in China and then there would have been money enough, we didn't need anyone to deal with the fact I was kicked out. Could I talk to her alone?"

Tom glared at him for a moment before he pulled BJ out of the room. "We'll get supper on."

"I wrote to your father when the letters I sent to your college were never answered. I wrote Harry when I was back in the US military and could guarantee the letter went through but never heard back. You never went in to pick up your dependent payments. What happened?"

"You left for China and about a month later father died. Then Pearl happened. Harry, me, and my grandparents were thrown in Manzanar, some of the first. They wouldn't let Harry out. That was all before I heard you had died. I sent word telling you everything, but I guess it never got through. After I got here your father got another telegram."

Brock held her to his chest. There were a lot of things he imagined since he saw her last. None of it what happened. "Please tell me you finished school," Brock whispered.

She curled even closer to him. "I finally convinced them to let me finish college, Mrs. MacLean sponsored me, swore I wasn't an enemy spy and I only had a few months left and was pregnant. I graduated with honors just weeks before they sent word you had died."

"Where's your mother, she would have gotten the ones sent to your family? They wouldn't have thrown her in a camp, she's as white as I am."

"She didn't remember us. Not even dad or Harry. I'm sure you noticed it coming on before you left, it went downhill after dad died. I put her in a sanatorium when they sent the word we had to go to the camps. She didn't know who I was. The house had been in her name to save it, but I had to sell to keep her cared for while we sat there interned. She died about 2 years ago."

Hell. This was a mess. But more of a mess when he knew what was behind it. Like the fact his father was a bastard. Hell. Destroying her bit of calm could come later. "You're the maid next door aren't you?"

Amy nodded slowly. "How did you know?"

"The private that drove me home told me I should go stare at the maid over there. I took a guess when I saw you. Why not just get your payments you don't need to be a maid?" If she'd been there since 1942, his father was dead.

"I was working at the Aberdeen Proving Grounds as a computer, all those bombing runs I was one doing the ballistics tables for the precision runs for about 4 months. I was making 2,000 a year at that point. Then I was transferred to a top secret office in late '42. They saw I was worth more than doing figures. 12 hour days, 7 days a week, BJ hardly knew me. But they snapped me up and I never came back to the West Coast to be sent back to the camps. I sent money to Harry and my grandparents to buy things if they could. I paid someone to take care of BJ. I didn't need it. And I thought you were dead, there weren't payments to collect."

Brock closed his eyes. "Amy, what happened? Why are you here?"

"Harry signed up when they allowed the men to get out and go fight in Europe if they wanted. He was a medical student, so they made him a medic. It's round about, but I'd been petitioning to get my grandparents out ever since I went east. Two months before they started emptying the camps completely because it was wrong, I get word they're free to leave. I took off work to come get them take them back with me and while I was on the train they got word Harry died at Biffontaine."

A tear fell down his cheeks. He'd always hoped he was safe in a camp at the most. In prison but alive. "I'm sorry."

"We endure what we cannot change."

"But that doesn't explain you here?"

Amy shook her head in silence. "When my grandparents heard the news it took my grandmother from the shock—she was dead the same day. My grandfather was still alive, but a broken heart at her gone. We brought her back up to here to be buried with her family; grandfather didn't last a week. I buried him next to her. I had at least one friend, she told me that the neighbor turned me in as a subversive because we were behind the arbitrary line. I could end up in prison just telling you I worked in DC, if it got back I was arrested for spying I'd probably be hanged. I got away and ran here. I've been hiding here since. I heard about you dying in China years ago and Tom gave me some hope when I got here that you'd sent a letter just a few weeks before, but then he got another telegram."

The bastard was lying for one thing. Brock hadn't written the man since the war started. Amy's hand went to her mouth in shock as Brock pulled out a ring. Burma during a war, the merchant was willing to sell it cheap so he could have money to flee. It was a stone for a princess. The ruby as large as a dime sparkled in the dull light. "I said I was going over there to treat you the way you deserved. I've carried that around for a very long time waiting to have you show we were married."

Finally she looked up at him. New tears slipped down her cheeks. "You promise I'm not dreaming that you're here."

"I'm not the man that left but I promise what's left of me is yours."

More tears fell. Maybe not all of life was gone. "How long are you here?"

"I was given a month."

Then she just held on like her life depended on it. "It's not enough."

"It's what I can offer right now. There's already talk of..."

"Yes. Japan," she finished. Her own father's people and she was caught in the middle. Quickly she was wiping the tears from her cheeks. "Then we'll have to make it the best month of your life."

His hands holding her face stopped her flurry of activity. "Trying to give you the best took me from you. Just give me a life to come back to."

"Life," she whispered.

Surely she couldn't see life in his eyes anymore. Surely he had bombed even that from existence.

Amy rested her forehead against his. "The minute this war is over you're promised to take me and BJ to the islands. We can't bring back the past, but we'll make a future. Don't say you might not come back, you've come back once already."

Brock couldn't keep the tears from falling.

"Shhhh," Amy whispered in his ear. "I'm sorry you ever thought you were alone. I'm sorry you never knew you had a son. I'm sorry about a lot of things. You never would have let me quit school; your father never accepted us. People died and moved that should have passed on news. I am sorry, Brock, you should have always known you were loved if a single telegram hadn't stopped me from sending letters. I know how many letters you wrote when we were in college, I can guess somewhere a woman living in an old rooming house is getting quite an education in naughty letters."

She was trying to cheer him up, but it would take more than that. "That isn't what I remember, it was sitting there in the dark talking, your head resting on my stomach long before I ever kissed you. I can hardly picture it anymore, my nights are filled with bombing now. I close my eyes and the world is gone."

Amy stood and held out her hand. Cheeks stained with tears beckoned him. He couldn't say a word; her hand closed around his and she pulled him out of the chair. Going upstairs she led him to the room he had as a boy. A large poster bed hanging with dark wool curtains, by the fireplace were two fantastic cranes green with verdigris. Art deco copper lamps, next to mission chairs, next to Lummi Indian carvings. His life around him and yet not. Things that had long been put into the back of his head. She locked the door and bent at the fireplace. The fire slowly grew as he watched it. Incendiary bombs grew as bright, even from as high as he flew. The world burning beneath.

Then gentle hands unbuttoned his shirt. "A month isn't enough to live without fear of dying."

CHAPTER 2

i.

Brock woke with a scream as bombs blew the world apart. The world around him looked all wrong as he opened his eyes. A gentle shade of nature outside overgrown with ferns untouched by horror slowed his heart. The view out the window was spectacular. Lummi Island, Orcas behind it, Eliza off it as well. To the south Fidalgo. Guemes, Cypress, Vendovi, Jack. The little tiny dot of an island, Chuckanut. Small clouds rose from the hulking shapes like 1,000 campfires rising to the sky. No devastation, no airplane dropping death from above. Slowly reality came back to him; he was in Washington far from the war. Breathing heavy, he leaned his head back again while his heart pounded hard. His dreams were all the same of late, not being shot out the sky; he'd given up on that long ago. Now he waited for the retaliation bombings. Someone coming to destroy the sense of calm the way he did to so many. That's how he ended up back home. He'd mentioned the dreams to someone, and two days later he was headed home.

Amaya lay in the crook of his shoulder, but she wasn't asleep. She had one of the numerous books that filled the library. No, looking close, the title 'Forever Amber' didn't sound like some dowdy classic.

"What time is it?" Brock whispered.

"Almost noon. I have work soon."

He pulled her up and shook his head. "No, you're quitting."

"But..."

"I'm not being a chauvinist ass. There are thousands sitting there in the bank from China, I lived frugally other than buying you that ring. That doesn't include what's left over from Air Force pay. Amy, there's something like 15,000 dollars in there. We just have to stop by and get you added back on as my dependents and you'll have more coming in than you're making waiting tables and still save that for when the war is over. If you're going to work then do something worthy of you. Don't just work because you need to eat. I'm making 4,000 a year base pay before allowances. They've been taking it out of my pay for you." Even if he thought she had left him.

Amy just stared at him. "So much?"

"Please, let me go back knowing you're taken care of after so long without it. If the airmen that come and stare are anything like the ones I serve with I don't want that for you. Work if you wish, but not that. We'll get your records cleared up. Please. I'll get it worked out."

Finally she started nodding.

Brock pulled a hair from her cheek. "I never thought a woman as beautiful and smart as you are would ever look at me."

"Is that why you never said anything?"

"Everything changed the day Harry said you wanted to come with him for the summer."

She straddled him, even laughing a bit. Leaning over, she grinned as she lay there nose to nose. "Didn't Harry ever tell you I begged after you came to dinner with him, a handsome, rugged, self-reliant man among boys. My grandmother loved you for asking her to make a full feast of all her favorites from home and then in the middle of no one having enough you sent around fish and crab enough to feed all of us for several days. You heard Harry saying they didn't have enough to eat until the harvest and that was a month away. Those old eyes of yours asking to draw me even if you never took advantage of me naked long before I had to ask you to marry me. You always

18

took care of me, from men that would have taken advantage to falling off a boat. Teaching me to swim and how to pleasure a man. My parents taught me how to be a farm wife and you taught me how to survive. You just looked at me and I would follow you anywhere, as rough and rugged as you are, you are a gentleman that never asked me to follow because I was Harry's sister. Thinking you were dead, my heart had been ripped out and it should never come back. That I gave you a son was all that made it bearable, something more than my memories of you survived. Never say that you aren't worthy of me."

Brock closed his eyes as she stole his heart all over again. "You've been here 6 months?"

"No, I didn't arrive here until December. It's been a little less than that. Why?"

Time to turn her world on its head. "Because something's wrong and I can't figure out what it is. We spent the summers on the boat because of him, Father is a racist ass and that was before Pearl turned sentiment against anyone."

Amy sat up, hand over her mouth. "Brock, tell me."

"I have a feeling that he sent you the telegram, what better way to get rid of a woman he didn't want. Nice and simple. If he had said he read it in the papers then yes it's doable, but not letters. He can't have heard from me to say I was alive, not when I never wrote. He didn't know we were married. When you showed up and there was a kid, he tells you there's another telegram. If your family is all dead there's no way to trace you and I give up looking. The house is sold, nothing to keep you in Seattle where I'd look for you. You'd be one of the thousands of war widows, married or not. Why would you look for a dead man? Why would I look for someone that left me?"

Tears ran down her cheeks in silence. "He didn't act like his son came back from the dead, did he? That's why he kept saying oh damn last night, he was caught."

"Not to mention that Mrs. Trevelyan didn't mention a thing about my being dead when she saw me yesterday. The woman knows everything going on around this town. If I was dead she'd have known. I'm sorry, Amaya, about so many things. I never wanted to tell you what he was like back then, I never wanted to ruin your summers knowing I kept you from a man that despised you."

Amy shook her head. "Then I'm glad you have trouble sleeping and came home off schedule."

"I wouldn't have, but I didn't know where my wife was. Here was at least close enough to take a bus down and look."

"But you said you can't figure it out. That sounds like a rather thought-through plan for not figuring it out."

"If he was the one getting you out of my life, then why would he keep you here? A lifetime of his tricks, I know he hasn't changed, but knowing what I do, I can't figure out why he let you stay."

Of all things, Amy smiled. "Brock, you might not have told me about his prejudice, but you told me the rest."

"Yes."

"Does he have money?"

Brock shook his head. "No, what he'd earned smuggling during Prohibition vanished the first couple years of the Depression." He stopped as he got the same idea she had. "If he found out we were married. If you think I'm not coming back he sends word to have your dependent checks come here. But that doesn't explain you staying here. Every day you're here it would be another chance more that he'd be found out. And those payments, they wouldn't pay for new bathrooms, kitchen, power, phone, electricity, water heater."

Amy stared. "Rationing wouldn't let him buy the fridge and such, the metal is scarce and no one makes them in favor of war goods. Those had to have been here shortly after you left, before the war and anything he could get from me. Yes that is worrying."

"Pack up your things and I'll get what I want to keep packed up before I go down. If I go distract him could you get it out to the car by yourself? We can get a room next door and keep it there. I still want to figure out what he's doing, but then we can leave without worrying. We'll have dinner over there after we get your mess figured out in town."

Amy ran her hands over his chest and the scar that marred it, a bullet that came through the windshield from a German Messerschmitt. It missed lungs and heart, just hurt like hell. The rest were all flak. His legs looked like hell. "How did you turn out the opposite of him?"

"You remember Mr. Campbell. I suppose because he hired me to help out at his place since I was small. He started showing me the world from this little tiny spit of land before my father could pass on his bile. He was an old missionary doctor in China, he was just as rough and tumble, had to be, working where he was, so he never minded that I could throw a punch or survive off the sea for months, even smuggling he didn't mind, but he never liked my father or his prejudices. When I was older, he saw I could draw, and he put me to work illustrating the book he was writing as well as tending the yard and running in with him to treat the workers in Chinatown. Only money we had coming in for a while. A 14 year old was supporting them all on a dollar a week, grandfather took clients when he could get them, but it wasn't regular and often it was paid in kind. When I got a little older I was fishing, lumberjacking, becoming the man you met when your brother brought me home. Father wouldn't work unless it was a scam to get him out of work. My mother started the chicken coop, but she was a well to do. Well brought up, a lady. She never worked, didn't know how. I'd never have eaten, let alone them, if I didn't go out like we had summers."

Amy kissed his chest. "Well where am I making a life for you to come back to when the war is over? That seems to be what we're talking about, isn't it?"

"I'm still getting over the fact you're here when I thought you were lost to me. I kept flying when I could have stopped, because you weren't anywhere I could find you. There was nothing to come back to. I'd asked if they heard anything here and nothing."

"You could quit right now?"

"While at war not really, but I could ask to be stationed here in the US. I've spent 4 years overseas no one can say I didn't spend my fair share. The war in Europe is on its final leg. Japan's the only worry about me going back. I'll see where things sit when leave is up."

"One worry at a time, I best get packing."

There was bread out and they must have made sausages for dinner the night before. Brock made a sandwich. He'd already carried out the largest trunk to the car.

"Married and you never told me?" Tom asked as he handed Brock a cup of coffee. "Where on earth did you do that?"

Did he know? It seemed that stealing 40 dollars a month wasn't the sort of thing he would do when he thought about it. "Court house out in Friday Harbor, figured no one needed to know until she was out of college. You had a fit so when the Tigers opened up I went over so I could earn some good money to support us while family disowned me. Hers didn't have anything to help. Harry becoming a doctor was their chance to get out of farming."

"He was my grandson and you never said he wasn't a ..."

"He's your grandson regardless of a piece of paper, and he sure as hell isn't a bastard." Brock snapped. "Where is BJ?"

"Out getting the eggs. Do you always wake up like that? I heard you several times last night."

Brock turned to the window. Some distraction he was giving. "Why the hell do you think I'm on leave? I flew my 85th mission the day before I left for here without more than a few weekends off in years, that doesn't count China. If all I have wrong with me is not sleeping well and a few scars, just remember most of the telegrams aren't mistakes." Brock sank in a chair and ate his sandwich.

BJ came running in. "There aren't any eggs."

"Damn little bastard, can't get nothing right," Tom said.

Brock put a hand on his son's shoulder. "Don't worry about it. If someone else needs them more, we won't grudge them a meal. BJ, go see if your mother is ready to go into town. We have some business to see to there."

"Yes sir." BJ ran off.

The anger grew and Brock turned on his father. "I wondered how long it would take you to show your true self. They were damn Japs long before the war started. You might have her convinced that you're a sweet old man, but I never want to hear you say something like that again about my son and you will never talk to him like that. Even if he was a bastard, it would have been because you made him one, nothing I did. I took the eggs last night when I got here and was starving." Brock went straight to the car, Amy had it ready to go.

"Can I see a plane you fly?" BJ asked in the silence.

"We'll have to see. I flew one in yesterday. I don't think it would have gone out already."

BJ started jumping in the backseat.

"But no asking to go up in one, they aren't for just taking up. We can definitely let you see one though."

The boy nodded even as he jumped around.

He turned into the Inn before he let out a sigh. Down a long track finally a clearing appeared overlooking the bay again. Mr. Campbell had planted dozens of cherry trees when he returned from China. The Cherry Blossom Inn was an apt name for the property. They were all blooming in tufts of pink everywhere he looked. "We aren't coming back."

"You gave up everything to marry me, didn't you?" Amy whispered.

Brock slipped his fingers in hers and kissed her hand. "I gained everything when I married you. Do you have ration coupons for clothes?" Brock asked instead. "I know Britain's rationing, I don't know here."

"They aren't rationed here. Shoes are because of the rubber. No silk stockings, sometimes I can get nylon ones. Styles are different to conserve material, but no outright rationing."

"Then we'll go shopping, you'll need a new dress for dinner." Brock got out and started pulling things out.

A stout man came walking out that Brock thought he recognized vaguely. A second cousin or something like that of a friend he had on the Lummi reservation.

"Smitty, can you get Jane to give us one of the cabins, biggest one she has. A week for now," Amy ordered before he could say anything.

"Sure, but..."

"I quit. My husband is home and three for dinner. I know my husband loves Mrs. Heinrich's Sahne Schnitzel. If she could have one made up for him since it's not on the menu. But we have some things to do in town before we settle in."

"I'll take your things over to number 15 then if you want to get the key from her. That one's out of the way."

Brock just drove them away; the winding road cloaked in mist grew silent. Amy seemed in shock as she took it all in. The bay was almost invisible beneath low-hanging clouds, and as they got closer it started raining. What else in Washington? Working his way through town Brock pulled to a stop for the trolley, and he was staring at a face he knew. Brock rolled down the window, only to be grabbed.

"When did you get back?" Greg Hartman asked, clapping him on the back. They'd been at school together. Good looking man, far too handsome a man, Susan had stared when Brock took her to the dance. A young Clark Gable with flashing green eyes was never good as competition. Greg was dancing with a friend of hers, they'd never gone out again. He was missing most of one arm now, had he been serving too and already wounded and back?

"I'm just here for leave, got in yesterday."

"Did you hear? The Germans announced Hitler was dead. Shot himself. The Russians overran the bunker."

"No, I hadn't."

"We have to get together."

"I'll be at the Cherry Blossom Inn if you're free tonight. Taking the wife for a night out."

"Great. Wait, wife?" Greg looked over, realizing Amy was there and winked. "There's no way that gorgeous creature ever deigned to let you marry her. Far too good for the both of us, I would think."

"5 years ago now."

Greg smirked, but a horn stopped any comments.

"7 or so."

"Sounds good." He ran off, shaking his head.

A few blocks further on Holly Street, Amy had him stop. "Why don't I shop for a dress while you're out there? You don't need me, do you, and keeping BJ quiet while I do it..."

Brock pulled out more cash than most had in a month. "Then have fun. Get as much as you want, or as much as they'll let you have anyway. I'll be back here in what? Two hours."

"Make it three." Amy hopped out with a wave.

She'd been a mother without fail for years even if someone else had to watch BJ in order to afford to support him, he'd give her anything he could afford at that point. The rest of the few miles to the airfield was uneventful. What was there to say, if he found proof of anything it would be that his father had been stealing from his wife and child. And that theory didn't explain anything really. BJ just spent the whole time jumping in place, waiting for the first sight of a plane.

Finally the flat plain not far from the sea came into view. Three runways crossed themselves, making a rough triangle. Some 30 buildings covered the outside edges. Many of them holding bombs, he'd heard.

"There they are." BJ cried as he spotted a plane coming in for a landing. "They're huge, you really fly them?"

"The B-29's are larger. They make those look like babies."

"Have you flown one of those, B-29's?"

Brock could only smile. "Just once as a co-pilot, they don't use them much in Europe. I'm in B-17's. Most of these are transport planes carrying goods to the Soviets." It wasn't the planes that bothered him, it wasn't the runs, he could still do those. It was the times between that bothered him, closing his eyes. Thinking about what he'd done. How many he'd killed. The Soviets were fighting a different war, from all he heard. It wasn't beating the Germans, it was taking all they could.

They got to the complex as the plane landed. Brock pulled to a stop and helped BJ out of the car. Brock bent to pick his son up and noticed boxes being unloaded from the plane. Not pallets that allowed millions of tons of goods to cross to allied countries, but small ones from the front of the plane.

"Sir. I wasn't expecting you today," Sullivan said from a hanger nearby.

"No, well it seems that my wife was waiting at my father's and presented me with a son. I don't suppose you'd show him

some planes—I need to talk to the records office people."
Sounded better than calling intelligence.

"You aren't telling me that the very same woman I was
telling you to go stare at..."

"I spent all last night showing her what you would like to
do to her. That's my wife you're talking about, I'll thank you to
get those ideas out of your head now that you know."

Sullivan smirked uncontrollably. "Who is this son then?"

"Brock Jr. BJ."

"Well then BJ, let's go see the plane that just landed."
Sullivan took him from Brock's arms and took him along.

Stepping in the office, Stephens jumped when he saw him
coming in. The boxes he'd seen coming off the plane were sort
of hidden behind the desk but not quite. It didn't take too
much of a guess at what he was doing. Black market probably.
An old hand at it, Brock knew a good set up when he saw one.
Planes running all over the country. It wouldn't take more than
a couple people to do it that way. Someone to shove some
crates in, someone to take them off. Two people might be the
whole operation.

"Sir?"

"Can I use the phone to contact the records office, DC?
The Seattle area intelligence office too?"

"Did you hear?"

"About Hitler, just now on the way here."

Stephens nodded slowly. "Looking to get out already and
the war's not even over yet."

"Until I hear otherwise I'm a Colonel in the Air Force
and my wife and child need to be provided for if I'm sent off
again. It's not over yet, and Japan's not close. I want to talk to
the person to fix it now. Or we can discuss your smuggling of
black market goods with them. I was learning how to smuggle
when I was a boy. You don't want to know how I could slip in
and out of here. Hell of a lot more sophisticated than letting the
entire airfield seeing you pull those boxes behind your desk off
the plane."

Stephens glared at him, gritting his jaw like he would want to kill him. "Kingfisher, get Air Force headquarters on the line or Seattle Intelligence office."

"Yes sir."

Brock poured himself a cup of coffee as he waited.

"You didn't have to pull rank," Stephens muttered.

"Then I did it wrong—by my accounts that was blackmail. Someone is messing with my life and I'm not going to sit around while some letter rots on a desk for weeks or months waiting for an answer."

BJ came running in jumping even higher than before. "Dad, one of the pilots has to run to Coupeville to pick something up. He asked if I could go with him. He'll only be gone about half an hour. Can I please?"

Brock half expected him to peer behind his mothers' leg, so shy he'd never talk to him. Taking weeks or months to ever think of him as father. It seemed telling a boy that a strange man was your father meant little if he could take you up in a plane. "He asked or you did?"

BJ lowered his eyes, caught.

"It's all right sir, I was telling him I need to make the run. He said he wasn't allowed to ask," a man said coming up behind him.

"Sir, your call to Seattle is going through, the one to DC it will be almost 2 hours before the line is free." Kingfisher called from the office.

"If I can take that first, we can both go with you if you didn't mind." Keep some sort of order in place. At least a colonel there with his son wasn't going to get anyone in trouble.

"No sir. I'm not done fueling yet. There's time."

Brock shook his head as BJ ran after the man.

"If you don't mind my asking, sir. How did you get ahead to become a Colonel?" Stephens said quietly.

"I didn't die when thousands of others around me did. Sitting here won't get you a promotion. I was First Lieutenant when I stepped foot in Europe, had my first promotion in months. I didn't get it by making sure I had the finer things in life tucked behind my seat when I was deprived of very little." Brock looked over his shoulder and the man shrank.

"Yes sir."

"Your call, sir. They're waiting," Kingfisher called.

Brock headed to the other room and took a deep breath as he picked up the phone. "Is this Intelligence?"

"Yes this is Agent McDonald, Colonel Harker. What can we do for you?"

"I need to check on a case for a woman called Amaya Kobayashi, she was in Seattle about 6 months ago, November I think it was. She was turned in by a former neighbor. I'd like to get the matter cleared up."

"Cleared up? It doesn't happen that quickly. But let me go find the file and see what we have."

Brock leaned back only to find Kingfisher watching him. "Your wife is Japanese?"

"Half. I went to college with her brother down in Seattle, they spent summers here for years before the war. She likes to swing dance, make candies and she's the smartest person you'll ever meet and she's the maid over at the Cherry Blossom Inn, so she's one of the most beautiful you've ever met."

Kingfisher's mouth opened quickly.

"I don't suppose you could think of a reason a man might keep around people he despises when they showed up."

"What?"

"I've been married since 1940, she went to finish college while I went to China. When we said we were engaged but not married my father had a fit, I was thrown out in point of fact. Then she gets word I died in China. Just about the time she finishes school and gets a job where I would never have an idea to look for her when I had good mail access. She had a bit of trouble last fall and came to a man that despises her, he let her stay. I only came here because I couldn't find her, and I thought Seattle was the first place to look. He's not the sort to let a woman and child he couldn't stand live there with him."

Kingfisher narrowed his eyes. "I would say for your life insurance, but seeing as you are alive that doesn't make sense."

"There's no case sir. You needn't have called." McDonald said in his ear.

"What do you mean no case? She wouldn't be hiding if there wasn't. She wouldn't be worried about being hanged for spying if there wasn't."

A silence came suddenly. "Oh Colonel Harker, this is your wife, isn't it? I see here she uses the name Amy Harker."

"Yes. I just got back on leave for the first time since the war started and she's hiding, working as a part-time maid because of this. She thought I was dead, because my family didn't approve and I couldn't find her because she'd left for a war job while I was in China. A spiteful neighbor called when she brought her grandmother back to bury her at home. She was going to bring them to the east coast, but they died instead. Next thing she's worried about the authorities thinking she's spying and going to be hanged if they catch her. I know she shouldn't have done it, but she thought I was dead and if she's gone our son is an orphan. If anyone thinks she's a spy then you're coming through me."

"I'm sorry about what's happened, but I suppose after what happened to her family and her own internment she wouldn't feel too secure waiting to be picked up, but there's nothing we have to accuse her of. There's record of the report, an agent looked into it, but she was cleared quickly. Since the camps were allowed to empty in January we let it go. We found her using the name Amy Harker, married name quite legitimate from before the war. Following that name, we found the same story you just told us. Her grandparents left the camps at long last, she came to take them east. They died and yes we questioned the neighbor. It seems that he wanted to get the farm but it was in her mother's name. When they did sell it sometime later it was sold at a profit to someone outside the community and he really got mad. The whole neighborhood knew about his prejudices. We closed the case after a couple weeks. I know she would have been tossed away a few years ago, but there have been court cases fighting that treatment against US citizens. We know we have a large population returning to the area, we have tried to be more understanding. There have been little to no true accounts of Japanese American treachery."

"This might sound odd but has anyone else ever called about her?"

"No, the file has been closed and untouched since it was cleared back in December."

"Thank you." Brock hung up slowly lost in thought.

"Sir, I might know what's going on," Kingfisher said quietly.

"Well spit it out."

"There's something going on at the Inn. Jane's got more black market goods there than you can imagine. An inn I might overlook it as wanting to keep customers but Bellingham is a liberty town, there's hundreds of men around on any given day. But it always seemed odd that they would go to this out of the way place. It's an officer sort of place, but it's usually filled with privates and seamen. Men that can't afford that sort of thing, she's all but giving it away."

"Shit!" Brock growled.

"You know what's going on?"

"My father's house is next door to the place and he thinks intelligence is looking at my wife for something. That call just said she's cleared of anything other than being half Japanese."

"But..."

"My father was one of the biggest smugglers along the coast here. He knows what's going on, he's part of it. He let her stay long enough to get entangled in whatever is going on there. Then he just has to call Intelligence and get her picked up saying she's hiding from another charge."

"He would do that to his own grandchild?"

Brock started throwing things in his head before he started throwing real things. "I dare say he would, especially when he hated Japs before there was a war making it patriotic. We dropped all our stuff at the Inn leaving his house thinking there was safe. God if only I had a car I could keep it there ready to leave whenever we wanted. The one I'm in is my father's. If I keep it much longer he'll probably call the police on me."

"Does that mean you aren't coming back here to stay then with your wife and son?"

"No, I doubt it."

Kingfisher dug in his desk and handed over ration coupons. "There would be 4 gallons a week with that. It's not much though, enough to keep a car from the motor pool going. I could let you have one if you provide the gas. Stephens is just trying to show you he's in charge. You outrank him."

"You want to bring it to the Inn in time for supper tonight, my treat for the favor. I have one here to get back. I ran into another friend that's coming, it's turning into a party it seems."

The man's face lit up. Stephens would never deign to have a meal with him, it seemed. Not that officers and enlisted were supposed to interact. "Yes sir."

iii.

Amy looked radiant as he pulled into the shop front. She'd clearly had her hair done, and a crisp pale green dress replaced the one she'd had on.

"I got to ride in a plane, mama," BJ called.

"You let him beg for..."

"They had a hop over to Coupeville, weren't up more than 15 minutes or so each way."

"Did you have fun?" Amy smiled as he got in and once more he'd have to turn her world upside down.

"We have some problems though. One is you aren't being looked for. They did look into you, but found the neighbor had it in for you when you sold the farm to someone else."

"I've been hiding for nothing?"

"I guess they aren't as ridiculous as they once were with it. They at least check things out first."

"Good lord," she whispered. "That doesn't sound like a problem though."

"I'll get to that. No one was stealing from you, they're sending along your payments for the last years, I couldn't get BJ's extra money since I didn't declare him when he was born, but there's enough coming to settle somewhere. Should be here next week. Kingfisher, the clerk out at the airfield, I randomly asked about why you'd be kept at a house you weren't wanted.

He said there's something going on at the Inn. Lots of black market goods."

Amy nodded. "Your father brings goods to her."

Brock turned quickly. "You knew?"

"I'm not blind. She has something going on, there's no way she should be staying open. Never has enough people there to pay for what she must for the black market goods. And what she pays your father for keeping his mouth shut doesn't help her books."

"He's blackmailing her."

"He got me the job there, if it's blackmail it's rather friendly. But I've seen her handing over money."

Brock stared for a moment. "That doesn't change what I think he was doing. If he wants you gone and he thinks they're looking for you. You had to have worked there for a while before he calls in the authorities to get you thrown away for good."

"You really think your father would want me gone enough to have me framed?"

"Unfortunately I rather think he would."

Amy stared out the front window and let out a sigh. But she said nothing. "Have you had lunch, BJ?"

"Yes. With real pilots."

"Your father is a real pilot. You want to go in the shop right there and pick out a sweet." She handed him a couple pennies. "If they want to know where we are, just point to the car." She watched close as he ran to the door and someone let him in. He pointed quickly.

"Amy..."

"I need to think. I've been working at the place; you'd think I would notice things."

"I got a car so we can put all our things in it, if we have to leave we can leave. Kingfisher will drive it out tonight to have dinner with us. We can't go far but we can leave."

She nodded faintly. Her mouth opened once or twice, but nothing came out. "I haven't a clue, what. But intelligence is there right now."

"You aren't joking with me?" Brock gasped.

"Normal uniform, but no rank insignia, just US. They came to the office now and then back when I was working in DC."

"That would be them," Brock muttered. "But if you were involved I'd have gotten some run around. They wouldn't have said you were pure as the driven snow. They had to have heard what facility the call was from, they'd have known if you were under investigation in the same town. I'd have gotten something like we can't say, it can't be cleared up like that."

Amy put a finger over his mouth. "But if Jane was being watched it makes sense." Her mouth fell open and just silence. This time she couldn't dismiss it. "Things have been going missing."

"Like what?"

"Papers, watches, jewelry. All sorts of things, most is found after a day or so, before the guest leaves. 'The maid must have moved it, I'll ask.' I'd never know but one man came and apologized for getting me in trouble when it was found fallen next to the bed. He said Jane told him it happened all the time. Not the finding it by the bed, but it going missing on my watch. I asked Mrs. Heinrichs and she said it was rather odd that it didn't seem to matter the maid, it still went missing."

Brock rubbed his face trying to stem the anger.

"Did I just say she's stealing papers from the military men that are there?"

"Isn't it just the men on liberty that stay there?"

Amy shook her head. "They come out for dinner and dancing, drinking, but few of them stay there. The rooms when they're being used are mostly higher ups. Majors, Captains, Colonels, Mrs. Heinrichs says there was even a General before my time. One of the men at the Airfield I think talks them into coming out for the evening. Most of the black market she gets it's not high end goods it's just more of the basics—sugar, chocolate, coffee, alcohol, cigarettes. She does get some high end things for the overnight guests, but most it's just what I mentioned. I help out Mrs. Heinrichs in the kitchen making desserts that have no rationing in place, lots of chocolate, sugar. The kitchen has it all."

"You always did like making treats."

"I made a chocolate mint cake before you arrived, make sure to get some tonight I can't make one at home without breaking the law."

"I'll do that." Brock went silent himself. "People in town know though, Mrs. Trevelyan said I should go ask Mrs. Heinrichs to give me groceries when she heard I didn't have any ration coupons. They did give me a month's worth when I was there today."

"I should have known. I should have seen it." Amy whispered.

"What, because you're more worried about your family gone, and no money, and BJ, and maybe sent to prison, if not hanged."

"I should have seen your father didn't want us there. Now that you said it I can see he didn't. BJ told me he said things and I didn't believe him because I couldn't imagine your family being so bad. You came from him. How could he be so horrible?"

Brock pulled her over to his shoulder. "Did you find something to tempt a saint?"

"Yes, but you'll have to wait."

"Good. I forgot what you looked like all dolled up."

"Is that your way of saying I shouldn't think about it?"

"That's my way of saying you've spent too long being a widow." Amy just grinned at him.

CHAPTER 3

With Amy and BJ at the Inn, Brock took the car back. His father stood on the porch glaring. A faint sun tried to filter through and failed, leaving dark shadows of trees highlighted in the white.

"Where have you been?"

"In town like I said I would be. We'll be over having dinner at the Inn. A man will be delivering a car to us there."

"You emptied the house out," Tom screamed.

"No, I took what was mine, little that there was fit in a trunk all told. You'd only know I took anything if you were snooping so I have to wonder what you were doing while we were gone. Amy's thinking of a place in town now that she doesn't have to hide anymore. I didn't see the point in bothering you any longer when you made it obvious you only had names to call BJ."

"What?"

"Oh I called while we were out, seems no one is looking for her. She was checked out and cleared months ago. It was her own worry that kept her here and with the money coming from her dependent money she can afford a place of her own. We'll be next door while we find her a place. Another nice thing they told me, there have never been telegrams sent on my behalf. It's hard to check China, of course seeing as I was there with them it's unlikely something was sent accidentally. There

35

weren't many of us to keep track of. The one you supposedly received at Christmas, now that one they could verify and it doesn't exist. I think you'll find that is the end of our dealings, father. I tried to have another chance and now it's ended any connection we had."

Dappled light tried to come through the canopy of trees as Brock walked the fern lined path, overgrown now but still visible.

"Brock you always were a bastard!" Tom screamed.

That was not the thing to say. "I can fly and I can smuggle with the best of them, but past that you have ignored me for most of my life. You don't change, you never have, so why should I put up with you pretending? How does that make me anything like you?"

His family house jutted out into the bay alone on the point. Cutting back into the interior he crossed over to the next point before threading his way back to the shore. The Inn was a massive Craftsman central building, old Campbell's house once. Tucked almost hidden among the trees stood a grouping of cabins in ordered rows overlooking the water, all painted deep green that blended into the shadows. The cabins were all laid out to give each a grand view of the water, they'd cut down cherry trees to put them in though.

A man stood there staring at him. He was nondescript in many ways.

"I suppose you heard the yelling?"

"Hard to miss. I don't think I've seen you around."

"No we just checked in this morning. My father lives next door, that's all the yelling is about."

"Oh I'm Roy Carlson."

"Colonel Brock Harker. What brings you to town?"

"Oh lord." A voice cried before there was an answer. It was Mrs. Heinrichs rushing out to grab him in a hug. She had to be 60 at least, a large big boned woman. She was the sort you expected to find on a farm, strong, hardworking, take no prisoners, but she had a huge smile for him. "When did you get in? When I heard someone asked for a special dish I didn't think it was you."

"Yesterday. I'm here on leave. I'll be here for a couple days at least, while we find Amy somewhere to stay until the war's over at least."

"Wait, you're BJ's father?"

Brock put his mouth near her ear. "Do you think she was staying at the house because she was a stranger? The better question is did I marry the girl 5 years ago as opposed to just having my fun."

Mrs. Heinrichs gasped. "She never said, I mean I guessed you were, but I couldn't imagine you doing that to the girl. So I figured I was wrong."

"No, the night we came for dinner with Harold that last time we'd just been married. Did it when we were sailing around up near Friday Harbor. Didn't tell anyone because she had to finish college, I was stationed who knew where, and by the time she'd done that Pearl had changed everything."

For a moment the woman stared. "But..."

"Father sent her word I was killed in China. When she showed up here he told her I hadn't died then, but got another telegram saying I had recently."

"The filthy bastard."

"Yeah, tell me about it."

"Except that wasn't what I was going to say. Mr. Campbell left you a legacy in his will."

Brock narrowed his eyes. "But his son?"

Mrs. Heinrichs nodded. "He got the house with most everything else and sold it immediately, he's down in Hollywood. Never wanted to do anything with some old Chinese missionary doctor's trinkets, he called them. Harold left all his Chinese things to you. He knew you'd appreciate them at least."

"Where am I supposed to put all this stuff? I left father's house, won't be going back. I don't have a room even other than some tiny thing at the airfield."

Mrs. Heinrichs grinned like an old devil. "Well, then you need someplace to live, don't you? Too bad you don't have a boat anymore."

"Didn't I just say that?" His mouth opened to say more. "You don't mean he left me the junk he sailed back home in."

"There you have it. Figured you'd appreciate it."

Brock could only stare. Harold was the one that pushed him to go to China and help the country he had called home. The money made up his mind though, but the idea came from Mr. Campbell. Harold was dead before Brock had left China. "You never told Amy?"

"Well like I said she never spoke of you, never said you were BJ's father. It's rather rude to go up to a girl and say by the way child did the boy I wiped the nose of go and knock you up before he went off to fight your own people."

"So father never spoke of her?"

Mrs. Heinrichs shook her head. "You mean that your wife is half Japanese, no I don't think he knew I had met her before the war. He never was seen in public with her, never took her to town. I guessed she was hiding here. Never said her name was Harker she was just Amy. You go get ready for dinner. I'll have a feast for you. After I'm done I could watch BJ for you if you wanted. If you're on leave you'll want to spend some time with that wife of yours. Might take you a couple days to get it back to form, but we'll get that boat cleaned up and you can get out of here. It's been docked for several years now. I don't think Jane will be happy with her former maid staying."

"Thanks. I took him up in a plane today, he'll probably have an early night he jumped around so much."

Mrs. Heinrichs just laughed as she waved him off.

"You just came from Europe?" Roy Carlson asked. Brock had forgotten he was there.

"If you were listening in and there is a call made to turn her in I'll have you know now they know all about her and it would just be spite."

"I wasn't..."

Brock looked over his shoulder. "If my own father would, forgive me for assuming everyone would."

ii.

Amy came out in just a robe as Brock slid the large trunk in the back of the basic black Ford Kingfisher dropped off.

"Hello Ma'am." Kingfisher said quietly. "Can I ask who is here so I'm not completely lost?"

Amy looked around. "Oh well let's see there's Mr. Poole, he's here trying to get over his estrangement with his daughter. She married a Marine and they weren't happy. Man's died so suddenly they're ready to make up. Roy Carlson he showed up yesterday, I hadn't learned much about him yet. There's a Lieutenant Kelti here with the Northwest Sea Frontier and his driver Charlotte Evers. He's rather stuck on himself, thinks he's Sam Spade but looks like MacArthur."

Kingfisher started laughing. "Is that all?"

"Magda Starek has been here a couple weeks now, she's hard to figure out. It's odd, I know she is from money but Jane's more of a snob. Petya Ivanov I'm sure you know him from the airfield. That's it."

"Well isn't this quaint," a new voice said. A woman.

The smile fell from Amy's face, the only guess it was Jane. The woman behind him was strawberry blond and in her 50's probably. A matronly woman, she was the sort he expected to see with 5 kids in tow. She was a good looking woman though.

"What do you think you're doing?"

"Quitting, last I heard. I'd think you'd want the business, you always are complaining about how little you make. Jane, this is my husband Colonel Brock Harker. The reports of his death were false, it seems. Brock this is Jane Briggs, the owner of the Inn."

"You're putting me in a tough spot tonight. There's no one to serve dinner. Magda doesn't like being inconvenienced. We've never had anyone like her here before, she's..."

"You can do it." Amy just pulled him to the cabin before Jane could answer. Scream would be a better word by the red hue her face had, the last Brock saw of it.

"Let us get dressed and we'll be over for drinks." Brock called to Kingfisher.

"I don't think staying here long term is a good plan," she whispered with the door closed. "I know there's not really anywhere to rent, I looked into it. I never meant to stay with your father long term."

She wouldn't mention possibly not coming back, the life that was gone returned he had asked for it. Brock kissed her forehead. "You were sleeping with BJ when I got back. Mrs. Heinrichs said Campbell left me the junk."

Amy just stared like he had. It had been too long, how had he ever forgotten how beautiful she was. "That's assuming the sails are useable after all this time. They were getting worn when we went out and that was 1937."

"It's livable at this moment, we can get it fixed up later unless you want to sit here with Jane snarling every time you show your face."

"No," she said immediately, not even having to think about it. "She was bad enough before I quit."

"That could even keep you busy when I have to leave again. Let me read of what you've done to the old boat. You are writing me this time?"

"Yes, Brock." Amy chewed on her fingernail for a moment. "Well if I'm doing all that I might just ask for more than a summer around the islands. I've never seen California or Mexico. And South America."

Brock just started laughing. "I guess that answers whether you're going back to work."

"We'll see where we stand at the end of your leave. I just found out you're alive—don't go sending me away just yet."

iii.

When Amy stepped from the bathroom Brock could only gape. A black dress showed off her breasts well, and then it flared out. She turned to reveal a keyhole back leaving far more flesh bare than he could have imagined in years.

"How did I ever catch you again?" Brock muttered.

"Mommy, you look beautiful."

"Thank you, my little man. What do you say we take your father over and show him how to dance again? He never was that good at it." Amy winked at him over BJ's head as he rushed to take her hand. He really never had been a dancer, she on the other hand could keep up with the best of them.

Campbell's house had been gutted when they reached it. Once separate rooms, all the interior walls were taken out, leaving just one large room up front, the kitchen and a private room ran along the back. All the character it had once was gone. When he turned there was a woman. A pretty blonde.

Several men stood around too. How civilized everyone looked as they stood around chatting. A war might not even be happening to look at them. Other than the uniforms it was the old days before the war.

"You don't see many here?"

Brock turned to the voice coming up from behind him. "What?" He was in uniform, air force. A woman hanging on his arm.

"Russians. I know that fellow he's the Lend Lease liaison for the planes that get shipped over to Russia from here. I'm Charles Greenly and this is my wife, Daisy. Just got here."

"Oh I like how that sounds, Charles." Daisy cooed.

"I couldn't get away from work though for a real trip so here we are."

Brock nodded faintly, not really caring to tell the truth. He was flaunting the airfield to a flyer as if it was the latest technology. "Congratulations. Pity about the weather, but you don't need a sunny weekend for a honeymoon, then do you?"

Daisy blushed prettily.

"Do you work at the airfield then?" Brock asked.

"Yes, wish I could have afforded more than this before I am sent overseas."

"Go enjoy your honeymoon." Brock wasn't going to make a promise that the war was over there. He could be reassigned to the Pacific regardless of the war in Europe. Same as he could.

Charles and Daisy took a drink from the sideboard tray and vanished.

"They aren't married so you know?" Amy muttered.

"Well it happens."

"You don't get my meaning. Almost every weekend he comes in with a new girl on his arm calling her his wife. He was stationed somewhere else and got in trouble for his wives, what the others mentioned was a general's daughter. They sent him here about the New Year supposedly to stay out of trouble. I think that's why they're all from out of town, he gets them to come visit from his old posting. He's not going overseas either. He's Air Technical Service Command working on a top secret something, only reason he's not cleaning toilets in Alaska is they need him close. He can't keep his mouth shut, but it's mostly lies."

Kingfisher came back from getting them drinks; Jane had decided they wouldn't get served with Amy quitting.

"Better your problem than mine," Brock answered.

Kingfisher just grinned. "Stephens's, not mine. He was not happy when he heard I was here and he wasn't." Greg had appeared and Kingfisher slipped him a drink, freeing up his hand. "There you are."

"John Poole." A man stuck his hand in Brock's face. He was a small rotund man, no one would expect him to fight, not in this war, he was probably even too old for WW1. Which certainly had to do with his eagerness to talk about it.

"Brock Harker," he said quietly.

"How'd you get out, Colonel?"

"Get out?"

"Hitler dead, FDR dead only a few weeks. I would think everyone would be hard at work."

"I assure you I earned it."

"Oh." He turned red.

"Did you forget how to dance, flyboy?" Amy asked before any more blathering came out.

"I'm not a big swing dancer, remember."

"Something to hold me tight on like we always did."

"Gladly. How about you take BJ for a turn first. I'd hate for him to think I'm stealing you."

Amy looked over her shoulder with a grin. "Well maybe he might. Come along, BJ, your father says you need to show him how to dance with me, it's been too long."

He rushed over, smile as wide as his face as Amy put on a record. That one was swing. The boy's giggle was infectious as Amy swung him around like a pro. The woman loved to dance. If anyone ever said a beautiful woman couldn't have a brain, they'd never met Amaya Kobayashi. Her not finishing school would have been a complete waste. She was a genius whenever he met teachers of hers. And that wasn't just being polite, she truly was when it came to math. Still in high school she got her brother through his college math classes for becoming a doctor.

"I don't appreciate you stealing my maid, and this is not an establishment for children," Jane said rather loudly behind them. "Bringing Indians to my place..."

"Then call the sheriff. It would be nice to see him again. Because I'll live with your annoyance no matter what the arguments. You'll survive."

She walked off without a word more.

"You shouldn't have invited me, sir." Kingfisher muttered under his breath.

"How did you know about what was going on here then?"

"She didn't know for several years, one of the men was joking about it and she heard. I was asked not to come back early last year. I rather thought she wouldn't say anything if it was as your guest." His eyes followed Amy.

"Do you mind my asking what tribe?"

"Cherokee."

"From back east then?"

Kingfisher nodded slowly. "Yes sir. She's good. Would you mind if I asked her to dance, sir?"

"Only if you think you can keep up with her. I never could."

The man walked off instantly. There was a new song starting and BJ gave her up reluctantly. Faintly he heard something about it was his dad's turn, but finally relented.

"How's life going?" Brock asked Greg.

He went back to the war instead. "2nd Air Force is in Italy, isn't it?"

"I'm with the 8th. When Doolittle rearranged things I was switched. North Africa into Italy with the 2nd, now England over Germany with the 8th. I was in England most recently." In the hardest raids on Germany until shortly before he left. That didn't count China. He'd cheated death so many times, he should be dead and he knew it. 5th Order of the Cloud and Banner from China, he was an ace with 7 kills, three more on the ground. Two Distinguished Unit Citations from missions he flew since, two Distinguished Flying Crosses for personal actions. It was nothing like what the men on the ground dealt with, he'd never say that. But life expectancy of a flyer wasn't great at times. He was an old man and not 30 yet. "I was sent on detached service and suddenly things are happening fast. I don't know what's going to happen if the war in Europe ends."

"Oh the notices in the paper before I was drafted mentioned the 2nd. I haven't read it much since I came back." He didn't have to explain more, all it talked of was the war. Too many friends dead. He surely had more to dream of than never crashing or being bombed.

"So I've always wanted to ask. Susan never looked at me again when she saw you at the dance. Anything ever happen?" Okay so it was a change of subject. He'd be standing there in silence if Greg returned to the war.

Greg turned and a little smirk spoke volumes. "Have you thought it was just an excuse to not see you?"

"And why would she have to run from me? It was the first time we went out and she ditched me about 20 minutes after we got there."

He leaned close so no one had to hear. "I never said she ran from you, she used you as an excuse to see someone her father didn't approve of. She came and talked to me about 5 minutes and vanished with a guy I was there with. If his boasting was true the next day Susan's father was right to worry. When you left for college she didn't come back for her last year, the Trevelyans said she went to live with an aunt that was poorly. I saw her up at a farm in Everson when I went to deliver for the lumberyard."

"You don't have to say the rest."

Greg nodded. "She's found a good man that's taken the kid as his own. I met them when they came to visit once. They're buying that farm up in Everson where I saw her, it did belong to an aunt. Money they're making at Bremerton can't be beat to get prepared for when the war is over."

A man in uniform and the blonde he'd seen earlier came over. She was hard not to notice. Pale hair, pale skin, milky blue eyes, only the deep red of her lipstick gave any color to her.

"Lieutenant Kelti with Northwest Sea Frontier and my driver Private Charlotte Evers," the man said.

Brock looked over briefly. He was certainly intelligence, he'd recognize the insignia anywhere, or the lack of it. Sea Frontier should have been Navy jurisdiction, not an Army driver. Someone wasn't paying attention. Brown hair longer on the top. The man would have looked rather like Hitler if he just grew a little mustache not to mention he smoked a corn cob pipe. Amy was right about looking like MacArthur.

"So how does a fighter ace with the Flying Tigers end up a bomber pilot over Europe? 7 kills, plus three on the ground. Now 80 missions." Kelti asked. Intelligence indeed. Kingfisher should have been the only one that knew of that or little old ladies that read the paper faithfully and Kingfisher hadn't left Amy's side.

"If you know that, you'll know how as well. I'd much rather have someone tell me something I don't know, like how such a beautiful woman is stuck driving cars for intelligence."

"For what?" Greg gasped.

Kelti put his pipe in his mouth and made a show of not caring. "Don't know what you're talking about."

"I'm from New Orleans just doing my part for the war." Charlotte answered, but not looking directly at him. All the proof he needed it was true.

The music changed and Amy held her hand out. A slow ballad from the old days. She just stepped into his arms and her scent overwhelmed him. As soon as he had his back turned, a woman he hadn't seen before surprised Greg by asking him to dance.

"You really wouldn't mind a boat instead of a house?" Brock asked.

"Why should I? I loved our summers. You taught me how to sail a boat and that one is easier than your fathers' to handle. Sometime in the future when the world isn't at war, I might want to settle down and be boring, but right now it's perfect." Amy rested her head on his shoulder. "You're worried about not coming back again and that's all there will be for us."

"I don't know that I can go back. Knowing they're only dreams is one thing, waking up like that again knowing it's all there is anymore..."

"Shhh," Amy whispered. "Tonight there's me, and tomorrow there's the boat and some flights, and in a while we'll figure out what to do when you've slept more than a night and aren't exhausted. When we see what Hitler dead means. You took care of me, now it's my turn."

There were others up dancing as well when the record arm was ripped off the disc. "Dinner," Jane called.

"Now she's just being petty," Amy muttered.

Jane looked even more put out as Mrs. Heinrichs brought out a tray with a feast as they sat down. Sahne schnitzel and spaetzle with asparagus, pumpernickel bread and German mustard. And pieces of the chocolate cake Amy mentioned. It was just for the three of them, the rest had rationing at its finest. If it had black market spoils in the pantry, there was no sign of it that night.

"When do I get that?" Poole called.

"When you were in Europe three days ago and haven't had my cooking since 1940 then I'll make it for the rest of you." Mrs. Heinrichs snapped and every face turned to him. "Sorry." Mrs. Heinrichs murmured under her breath. Somehow Mrs. Heinrichs had enough of everything that the food tasted just like it did the last time she cooked for him. Another man could have sat there it seemed so long ago.

Kingfisher looked up and his face fell. Brock turned quickly. Stephens stood there looking resplendent in his dress uniform making it very clear Kingfisher was nothing.

"I thought it was a poor greeting for you to have dinner on your own in a new post." He just came and sat down without asking. "Oh that looks wonderful."

"It's all gone." Mrs. Heinrichs muttered as she put a plate out for him. The same veggie meal that the rest had.

"What's this?" Jane asked. "We have more..." Maybe at the last minute she realized she shouldn't say it out loud.

"We're out until we can get more rations."

Jane looked up at her. "Oh. Yes, I'll have to go to town before dinner tomorrow. I forgot you told me."

Mrs. Heinrichs rushed back to the kitchen leaving Jane to serve the others.

"Dad, are we really going to live on a boat?" BJ asked.

"I guess so, seeing as we have one and nowhere else."

"Well no problem, a drink will make up for it." Stephens said and Jane rushed off to get him a Scotch.

Greg looked up quickly. "Boat? Where'd you get that?"

"Mrs. Heinrichs said Campbell left his old junk to me. I don't think the sails are worth anything, but we can spend my leave there other than the flights assigned to me."

Greg took a bite slowly. "You want help? I'm just sitting around, all the jobs are building war goods and missing a hand that isn't too easy to do."

"So what's this I hear you were just in Europe?" a fabulously dressed European woman said, bringing her plate and dragging a chair over. She looked like nothing he'd ever seen in Washington state, she was the one that had asked Greg to dance too. A teal feathered drape studded with sequins covered her hair highlighting the rope design that edged the full length white gown. It wasn't a daring dress, but neck to floor, long sleeved in just fabric, it was lavish compared to what most wore in Britain.

"I am Magda Stárek," she said rather dramatically in a thick accent.

"Czech?"

"Ah you know my country," she cooed.

"No, not really. There was a Stárek I flew with, he joined up after he fled the Germans."

"Who was that?"

"Vladen."

She nodded slowly. "Yes, the same family. My father he was in the old government. Ambassador to China until it fell to the Japanese."

Brock tried to bite his lip to not say anything. If he was right he'd heard of her when he was over there, orgies, drugs, mistress to a warlord even, if the gossip was right. Shanghai had fallen only a couple years before the Flying Tigers started up. Europeans especially ones that made a big name for themselves stuck out. Stárek must be a married name, it was surely the ambassador's daughter Magdala he'd heard tales of. Of course there was another daughter too. She'd married a Czech Prince and he was the Stárek. That was Magdalena. She was hiding something then.

Amy leaned over to his ear. "What are you smirking at?"

"Was I? I was trying not to. I'll tell you later."

"Brock..." Greg whispered.

"Sure. I'm guessing we'll need to scrape a lot after this long, paint. Of course before all that it will just be cleaning. I doubt there'll be the material around to replace the sails until the war is over." Brock answered before anyone could interrupt. Greg sounded rather lost frankly. Not messed up mentally at least not on the surface, he just didn't know where he fit in. No job didn't help. The same as he had been, not knowing what happened to his wife, only he had a job. Only his job was destroying the world beneath him.

"What kind of boat is it?" Magda asked.

"A junk actually, the man that used to own the house where we're sitting was a missionary in China. He escaped the Boxer Rebellion in it. I grew up just next door and I guess he left it to me when he died."

Magda looked surprised. "You know about China?"

"I was stationed there for some months with the Flying Tigers."

"You should see his record." Stephens jumped in. "A flying ace, and a bomber pilot, decorations and..." He faded off when he caught sight of Brock's frown. "Oh. Yes, I suppose you don't want to talk of the war. You know I could put in a request that you be given command of Coupeville, Whidbey Island, there are several right here that would be tranquil after Europe and North Africa. With the talk of the war in Europe ending soon why should they waste time sending you back. All the boys here can do that. Just give them all the tricks you've learned or would you not want that?"

Brock just sat there in shock. "I haven't really thought about anything frankly."

"You could be here all the time, Colonel?" Magda asked. "I have so little to do."

"Oh I think Madame you could find something to do wherever you go. I don't think I'm your type, not high profile enough at all."

Magda grew silent. "You know who I am?"

"One doesn't go to China and not hear about the Makovec sisters. Even in the middle of nowhere that I was stationed to not hear I had a son we heard tales of your renown."

She pulled out a fabulously long cigarette holder and Stephens held out a lighter for her. Her long lashes almost hid that she stared at him. Her eyes were as blue as the sea. It was no flower before him as she let out a long stream of smoke. A femme fatale in a movie picture surely. She smiled a seductive smile as she grabbed a drink. "I'm sure the stories about me have been greatly underreported."

"Then just how big was the brothel you ran? I heard hundreds of women."

Stephens spit out his next sip and stared at her in shock. "You heard what?"

"Oh the mistress of a Chinese warlord, opium by the pounds and orgies with priests."

Amy hid a grin in her napkin. She knew exactly what his smirk had been about.

For a long moment there was nothing then Magda started laughing. "Well there were never any priests involved."

iii.

Mrs. Heinrichs took BJ to bed after dinner when a busload of men on leave came pouring in. Suddenly the whole place was full, and loud. A complete opposite of the sedate inn they had checked into. Not a place for children indeed. If Prohibition was back on it was little better than a speakeasy. A long dirt track on a spit with no other houses in some distance, what better place to hock rationed alcohol. No donuts and coffee at a canteen. They seemed to have it all. There was a man serving as bartender, and women...

"Brock, why I haven't seen you in ages," one of them said out of the blue. One of his father's birthday presents. Good lord what was she doing there.

"No, I've been away since '41. Married since '40."

The woman turned her head slowly as she realized Amy was there. "You putting me on, Brock? No one brings their wives..."

"Your friend is getting annoyed." Brock said instead.

"Oh yes." She ran off.

"You mean all of them are prostitutes?" Amy muttered.

"You didn't know?" Brock whispered.

"When they bring in their shipments, your father didn't want me anywhere near here. I never worked, I never was invited. I would serve dinner and told to get the hell out of here. Not quite that bluntly, but the same idea. I enjoyed it. I knew Tom would be gone all night and I could just put BJ to bed and have a night to myself."

Brock kissed her neck. "Never looking for a serviceman to replace me."

"If you knew how many offers I had to replace you, you wouldn't be so flippant about jokes of that nature."

"I was dead."

"But not buried. I rather hoped it was a mistake, then I got here and he says you're dead recent, not years before."

"Come on." A man pulled Amy off to dance.

"Abandoned, Colonel?" It was the first time Petya Ivanov had spoken to him. He was tanned with pale, pale blue eyes and sharp features.

"When she starts dancing, almost always."

"Decadence."

Brock looked over getting angry. "Then what are you doing here, drinking, dancing, partying? Looks like a proper evening to write home about to people starving."

"Ah there you are, my dear man." Magda swept over and hung on Petya's arm. "What are we talking about?"

"Decadence, it seems my wife dancing is against communism."

"I never said that sir, I like decadence. It is so much more colorful than Russia."

Brock felt a little warm under the collar. "Oh. Then I am sorry."

"Petya is from Ukraine." Magda added. "He's a beautiful author if they would let him be and not farming or whatever else it is they force them to do."

He started laughing. "I could never be here to meet a beautiful woman in America, I could be on the Eastern Front. I could be in the Gulag again."

"Again?" Magda gasped.

"I was heard joking about the government. I guess they are lacking people with an education to run things though I never expected to be given a government position, never sent somewhere else to serve it."

When Brock looked up the man that had pulled Amy to dance had his hand running along her ass. He knew she could take care of herself, but when he pulled her close that was it. Every step across the room he didn't even seem to care it was a room full of people, Amy opened her mouth to yell and he kissed her. She got her knee up, but he was too tall, he just pulled her closer. Brock put a hand on his shoulder.

He looked up angry, ready to argue a defense for attacking her in view of the room.

Brock put his weight into it as he slugged him hard. Several of the other men who must have been friends of his started to join in until Brock straightened up. It faded as they saw who he was. "Colonel..."

"Get out! I don't care who it is, I ever see you treating a woman like that again and I'll take this uniform off and tear you apart. The fact I had to watch it with my wife..."

"She never said she was your wife..."

"Seeing as you had a dance together I don't see a reason she needed to tell you. I expect you to have some consideration past fucking anything that wears a skirt after 2 minutes. You and your friends will leave now or I'll have the lot of you brought up on charges before you ever make it back to station."

They helped the man on the floor up and started for the door.

"If he'd ever been overseas he'd understand," one muttered but in the silence it was loud enough.

Greg stepped in front of the doorway. "Apologize."

"What? A civilian would talk to me like that."

"You think I got this damn arm felling timber. I said apologize. The man you just said couldn't understand hasn't stepped foot in the US since 1941, before Pearl Harbor. He was in China fighting the Japanese, an ace, before going to Europe to spend the next three years flying 85 bombing runs. He is a damn Colonel because he survived the worst of the war in the air, shot down more than once. He didn't come back to go on publicity tours when he got 25, or train others. He'd already done that when I joined up and left my arm at the Bulge. The brother of the woman you just thought attacking as your right died in France, a medic that went out to save several men wounded when the Germans came up on them. He threw himself on their bodies, he saved their lives by giving up his own. They gave him a star for dying so well. Now seeing as I heard one of you mentioning you were just out of basic three months ago and you haven't been overseas yourself its time you understand, I said apologize and heaven help us if you're the best we can throw at them. Missing home isn't enough of a reason to attack a woman like that, married or not. I'm saying that because I know the Colonel, know he was wiping the floor with kids like you when your mama was still wiping your nose. Make any more stupid cracks like that and you'll find that old man will teach you a lesson and he won't call the cops or the MP's to do it."

"Sorry sir, he's been raring to get out and fight. I suppose he's a bit worried it will all be over before he gets there. Ma'am deepest regrets." It wasn't the attacker that said it, but one of the others that was about to come to his rescue. He dragged the others out the door.

Amy reached up and kissed Greg's cheek. "Thank you."

"Ma'am if you aren't tired yet," Kingfisher asked. "I would love the next dance," he said before she had a chance to even dwell on being pawed.

iiii.

Brock sat out on the porch hours later. Kingfisher wasn't giving up a dance partner if Amy was still interested, to the envy of all the newcomers. Or was it Kingfisher wasn't one of the strangers, he hardly let her out of his sight. The man was good. Mist hung in the darkness, making everything damp. The few lights that flooded from the windows couldn't penetrate it. Months of mist and rain punctuated by glorious summers. That was Washington life; it was different from English rain somehow. Maybe just that it was the rain of home.

Magda sank next to him. The fancy dress was gone; she just had on pants and a sweater now. "You know who I am?"

"I figured if you're going to play a part I didn't need to shout it out, Princess. Vladen talked intently of his cousin's wife that was in the Resistance and of his cousin's death a few years ago. And the son that had to be slipped out of where he was living. That was before I met him though. I can't say I ever expected to meet you here."

"So much for secrecy."

Brock grinned faintly. "Well he might be a little loose-lipped. But there aren't many that have heard. I think he only tells those he's trying to impress, like colonels. He could care less about privates."

"Sounds like him. He always was the worst social climber. My son, Augustin, he is staying at a castle in Scotland. The home of an old friend. I've been based there since '43; he deserves a mother. Thank you for keeping my identity quiet. I don't need men like Stephens brown nosing."

"You're playing your sister though?"

Her grin said it all. "No one expects a complete slut to know anything, most don't know she died. The world has been in chaos for a long time and my father didn't want to announce how she was found. Did it make it around she was sleeping with the Nazis when Father was posted there before China? I was kept in a Catholic school with vicious nuns to make sure I never turned out like her."

"You should get to bed, or is it just me that is exhausted? I can hardly keep my eyes open."

"What's Greg's story before I do?"

"I don't know. I haven't had the heart to ask, maybe I just don't want to hear the details. That comment about the Bulge was the first time he's hinted even. We went to school together, same class. His father worked at a lumber mill and knew he was damn lucky to have the job during the Depression. Mother took in laundry. He worked part time at the hardware store while he was in school. Should have gone to college if they had the money for it, he'd have done well. I haven't seen him since '40 until I ran into him in the street today."

Magda stood and kissed his forehead. "It's worth it. Just remember that."

"I suppose you knew of the camps long before Bergen-Belsen was found, with your going home to help all the time."

She nodded faintly. "I helped a man that escaped from Treblinka get out of Europe and into England. I spent several weeks interviewing him. No one believed what I reported. Not much could have been done even if they had, other than winning the war."

"Are you here officially?"

"No. At least not any more. Getting back to England isn't the easiest to do these days, I figured I might as well sit here as in New York until the ship leaves. I have a contact down in Oregon, he has a house I could use, but sitting there alone just seems depressing. I'll head out in a couple weeks and make a big splash there just before I sail. The Prince was poor and being his widow isn't cheap. Sitting here for a month as Magda, means I can be the Princess there for a night or two. It helps hide the woman that sneaks back into Prague rather well, I must say."

Brock dug out some bills from his pocket.

"I can't...that wasn't a plea for money. I have a Duke and an Earl that are helping me play the part and the Earl's richer than sin. I use their houses in London, Bristol, and Scotland to keep up the pretense, and a Hollywood contact gives me old movie dresses."

"I told Amy today she'd been a widow long enough. That's for Magdalena to go do something for herself. Your husband wouldn't like knowing you lost yourself in avenging his death."

Her shoulders fell. "You sure you didn't know him?"

"Go do something for Magdalena. When this war ends there has to be something of her left."

It was the grin of the part she was playing, sort of, that grew on her lips. "What I want to do for me doesn't take money. I've only ever slept with one man."

"Amy will beat you up if you say you want me to fix that."

Magda kissed his forehead again. "I'm sure she would; after that speech it's no wonder she's pined for you all this time. You can tell me one thing though, would a man think me too forward if I went and told him I wanted him to fix that."

"You're asking that, knowing who your sister is?"

"I told you, father all but kept me prisoner worried I'd end up like her, I married as a virgin to a virgin with no clue what he was going to do that night. Now I'm a widow and no one cares..." She shrugged her shoulders looking rather embarrassed she even had to say it.

"He'd think he died and went to heaven if you whispered that in his ear. Pity I'm married."

She just nodded and walked off. The rain was picking up from mist to steady. Wind whipped through the trees, it was no wonder Magda had changed to something warmer. A right storm was working itself up.

"I should get back," Kingfisher said out of the night. "Before your wife has me enchanted and you're fighting me over her."

"I just realized, how are you getting back? Stephens is being an ass, playing Captain."

"At least you said it, I'd be on report if I said that. Greg will take me. He wants to make sure he rests up for work tomorrow. You knew that asking meant a lot to him, didn't you?"

Brock nodded slowly. "Same as it would be me asking, only I have to worry about being sent back."

"I'll send in your request for somewhere around here then. Stephens makes the promises, I do the work. I can't promise anything though. If Europe would end I might be able to get you out altogether unless you wanted a desk job somewhere, I wouldn't give up the pay, but that's me."

"I joined up to fly—it's the one thing I'm good at other than surviving."

"Why didn't you put in papers before?"

His eyes closed slowly and the nothingness returned. "If your family made your wife think you were dead, would you be running back with open arms? If your family made you think your wife had left you, would you come back?"

"No I suppose not. Please don't tell me you were hoping to get killed."

"I am a Colonel because I didn't die. I get scratches while the men around me are torn to shreds. I gave up on dying a long time ago and now I close my eyes and there is nothing, a plane falling endlessly because I've blown the whole world to pieces so I can never land, and I run out of gas and fall forever. My life is back, but the dreams don't leave."

There was no missing Magda suddenly running through the rain, no mistaking Greg alongside her either. Well maybe he shouldn't expect him first thing the next morning.

"Maybe I'm not getting home that way," Kingfisher muttered. "It's already midnight. Stephens will kill me if I don't show up, when he knows I was here and he wasn't invited."

"I can take you in, Corporal," Kelti said from the door.

"Could you, sir? Let me get my hat. And with that I'll leave you to your wife. Thank you for sharing."

Brock looked over. Amy had found him. "You all right?" she asked.

"As much as I would love to..."

"You need sleep?"

All he could do was nod.

v.

A huge crash woke Brock in the night; this wasn't a dream, his dreams never ended in crashes, just endless falling. And it was close. The wind outside was nasty as it buffeted the cabin, rattling the windows. He must have been exhausted to sleep through it. When he looked out the window, the trees were swaying dangerously. He could hear them creaking even over the gale.

"What was that?" Amy moaned half asleep still.

"I think a tree fell. The storm got nasty."

"Hopefully we won't have another landslide."

"Is there anything right around us that could get hit? It sounded close."

"Cabin 14 and 16, these three are by themselves."

"Is anyone in them?"

She was waking up finally. "Oh I see what you mean. No we're alone this far, she doesn't fill them often, just come back to bed. There's little to do until morning."

CHAPTER 4

Brock stared at the ceiling after waking with a start. That was a dream.

"She's very beautiful," Amy whispered.

"Amaya, if I was interested in any other woman, I would have fallen for one when I thought you had left me. When you were thousands of miles away. It would have happened long ago, not under your nose. Whatever you think you saw, it isn't what you think."

"She knows about Europe—all I can say is what the papers report, and Harry's letters."

Brock kissed her head. "Yes even with that. Go back to sleep. It's still early, and you were dancing half the night."

Walking outside, he thought a bomb might have hit, with the damage. The wind still blew, but nothing like what it was in the night. Branches littered the grounds. Then Brock turned; the cabin next to them was demolished. A huge root ball rose in the air behind their cabin; the top of the massive tree brushed another cabin rather far away. The whole hillside had been logged once; the cherry trees had been planted to hide that fact. A few trees had missed the saw, those were massive now as the hillsides grew with smaller ones. That wasn't saying much though; some of those were taken 40 years ago, and their replacements were 60 feet tall already. Helped along by getting some trees planted during the Depression by his grandfather, hoping to help stop some of the landslides. An idea he got from the CCC. Grandfather had him plant the trees though; Harold paid for him to do his too. Huge tufts of pink flowers that had greeted his arrival were gone, blown away in the melee. His grandfather was determined he'd go to college. No running off and becoming a hobo, he wasn't really old enough to do the official CCC. He worked to feed them all, that was the thing about the sea being so close. They were never without food but it took work, and his father didn't work. It was left to him. What jobs he could get helped out so that the money remained for him to go to school. He was an odd one in that.

Roy came out rubbing his eyes, and they went huge at the treetop almost on his porch. "I thought I heard something in the night. Damn."

"Where's Smitty? This is going to be a mess to clean up," Mrs. Heinrichs muttered as she wandered around the grounds. "I'll have to find some men in town to come help. He'll never get this all done himself."

"You'll be set for firewood for years," Brock added.

Mrs. Heinrichs just grinned. "Where is Jane? You'd think she'd be out here surveying the damage, it's her inn."

"Will breakfast be on? I'm famished," Roy asked.

"They'll be a cold breakfast this morning I'm afraid. The power to the main lodge is down from a branch. It's all set up in the dining room when you're ready. Brock, if you can wait until I'm done with breakfast I'll show you the boat."

Brock helped pull branches out of the way while Amy still slept, and got ready. He couldn't just sit there, not while it looked like a bomb had gone off. Not while...

ii.

It was a convoy that went up to town and found the docks. Greg was already sitting there though.

"When did you leave?"

"When the tree fell down in the night, I figured I needed to get out before the road was blocked by tree or landslide. That was about 5 this morning. I have a friend that needs to be looked in on, he's not getting on well. I try to make it over once a day. I can't find the boat though. We went out on it, didn't we? That trip I took with you, I didn't think I needed to ask what it looked like," Greg called.

"It's right there." Mrs. Heinrichs pointed to a -- well, it wasn't the junk Brock had sailed around a summer or two. This boat called Night Rain was twice the size; yacht was a better word. It was up in dry dock at least, not being left to the water for years. Stored well enough the storm the night before hadn't even bothered it. There was nothing Chinese about this boat however, other than the masts seemed to be set up for junk rigging.

"Mrs. Heinrichs..." Brock started.

"Well, Jane is an old friend of Harold's son, if she could hear me, I didn't want to tell you that Harold wanted to take another trip before he died. Harold was 80 already and found the old junk was rotting away. So he had this built. His son would never fight over that old rotting hulk he knew about; Harold never told him the plan because he would have said he was too old. He wanted to ask you to come with him and sail the world. Amy and Harry too. He wanted to be comfortable though to go around the world."

"It's worth a fortune..." Greg muttered.

"I can't say that it will win a race, but it's ever so roomy. They had delivered it just a few months before he died. I hid the papers for it and just let Harold's son think it was the old junk he left you. It's not quite finished."

Brock let out a groan. "It is livable? That was why we're here."

"Oh yes it's livable, 4 double berths, 1 single, he even had an office sort of space for him, two heads, there's a built in table and bench seats, all the furniture you'll need. All his Chinese trinkets he brought back are stored, ready to be put in when he had it finished. It will need a thorough going through after sitting here for several years. The sails are there but not rigged up. It still needs work, but it's cosmetic work on a new boat, not a 100-year-old rat trap. The second interior hull of the other one was failing. It would have needed a complete rebuild to even make it seaworthy. This was his dream boat. He wanted one last adventure with you there to do all the work, and he would finance it. He knew you were kicked out and unlikely to ever be let back into the fold. He wanted to leave you something. Your father's will leaves the house to some organization I can't remember the name of. It's not you even if you are the last ones. I have Aftermath meetings with the lawyer's wife, she came in fuming when she heard about it. You disowned and the only good one left. I brought some sheets for you and a few things I had extra. It wasn't much though."

"That's all right."

Mrs. Heinrichs pulled out a set of keys and handed them over. "You'll need to go to the lawyer and sign some things when you get a chance. Well go see."

BJ didn't need to be told twice, he sprinted up the plank and ran around the back deck until the door was opened. She was right about it needing work. The interior had crates sitting around with who knew what. The boat was larger than anything they had before. 60 feet at least, but it felt huge, three of them had squeezed into 27 feet before, and that was for months. Built onto the deck were narrower rooms: the dining room, galley and wheelhouse; out back was a covered deck. There was even a built-in table and benches. All were wood stained to look like teak; they surely weren't real. They could sleep and cook.

Mrs. Heinrichs pushed past and started rummaging through the kitchen. She wiped out cabinets and sink as they explored the rest. Below, there were 6 rooms, 5 with beds. They were small, but beds and closets would let them unpack, then a bathroom with a small shower. All of them were off an all-wood hall down the center. And one a desk and bookshelves where charts lay around for a voyage around the world, left by an old man not ready to die. The Pacific, Mediterranean, Atlantic, Caribbean, Harold wanted to see it all. Behind all that was the engine room for backup and storage. It wouldn't be a bad boat to live on, not like he was expecting. More than double the size of the one before.

"What's first?" Greg asked as they came back to the main deck. "Is there a hose anywhere so we can fill the water tanks? You have a generator too, I don't see any lights though. We can stop by that marine salvage place and pick some up."

"We'll empty everything out. Then we'll clean it from top to bottom. First priority is two berths along with the kitchen.

Amy, you want to go see what you can find in town to cook with." Even as he said it Mrs. Heinrichs was putting the contents of a box she'd brought into the cabinets. A jar of her famous cherry jam from the trees at the Inn and some coffee. She'd lived with a boat man, she put cubed sugar in to save making a mess. Everything was in tins or glass jars of all sorts. It looked like she had raided the kitchen of the Inn. Rice, noodles, jam, relish, everything she could put up they had a jar of, salt, pepper, hot sauce, pickles. Otherwise there was a pan, some random utensils and little else. If the drives for scrap were any indication, there wouldn't be much lying about anywhere in town. He'd heard piles of goods filled a field in town.

"We aren't going to move in now?" BJ pouted.

"When the winds die down enough to move it. We can get things done while we wait. You want to go help your mom get what we need so we can make lunch here. We need energy to work."

"Yes sir." BJ pulled Amy away without giving her a chance to talk.

"You don't want me making the beds?" Mrs. Heinrichs asked.

"I didn't see any down there when we were looking around."

"Oh goodness, I was just thinking of you getting settled. I didn't think about it not being finished. Right, let's pull everything out so we can scrub. Greg, why don't you go get some paint while we do that. This whole boat is wood; it's rather like living in a coffin. We can brighten it up at least. I just know that Jane was not happy last night, and I think you're the reason."

"What color do you want?" Greg asked.

Brock just stared. "Go hurry and ask Amy. Get some varnish so we can touch up if needed but ask her and get some white in case we need to touch up the exterior after I get these railings in place, before we put her in the water. I don't have brushes or anything so we'll need supplies too. There's no hurry. This storm needs to clear out before we can get her in, not to mention find beds." He handed him some cash and Greg ran. Whitecaps still washed over the docks nearby.

"You don't have to steal out of Jane's black market goods to fill the boat."

Mrs. Heinrichs shrugged. "Someone who needs them should get use of it. The woman could supply the town from our larder. Doesn't matter if I tell her we're full up and there aren't guests coming. She doesn't notice it's gone. Doesn't even keep track of what goes in and out." She turned suddenly. "You know?"

"Mrs. Trevelyan told me to come get supplies from you when she heard I didn't have ration coupons, before I even got to the house. I figure my father is her supplier. He's never done an honest day's work in his life."

Mrs. Heinrichs started laughing. "Nothing gets past her, does it? Or you."

"Who better to know his ways than the one he taught to follow in them? Where does he go, Seattle?"

"There, but he has some friend in Vancouver too. They take one case of everything on a ship that comes in, just enough that it could be claimed miscounting if anyone questions the number. I saw some tools here. You can get those rails up."

iii.

The boat was empty when Greg got back. He started going over the hull to make sure that it was fully covered after years of sitting there. It had been stored properly though, a few minor touch-ups were made by the time Amy returned. Mrs. Heinrichs had to get lunch on at the Inn, though; she'd gone back, leaving Amy to get the wood stove heated for dried split-pea soup and cheese sandwiches.

"What color did you find, Greg?" she asked as they sat down.

"They had a red I thought sounded like what you wanted. There was white like what was used on the exterior originally so you can touch up that too. Varnish for all the wood, brushes, cleaner, some tarps. I saw a crew at the shipyard going on lunch, they said they'd stop by and help us get her in the water tomorrow. The wind should have died down."

"We need mattresses before we can stay, not sure even tomorrow we'll have those. There's no wood to cook on other than some sticks that Amy picked up. I left my father, and no, I'm not going to patch that up. Jane now is offended because Amy quit, it seems. I don't want to just move every night, if there wasn't a war on I'm sure we could do this in just a couple days, but right now..."

Greg rested his chin on his fist, staring at his bowl.

"So how was last night?"

He lifted his eyes. "How'd you know about that?"

"She asked me if a man would think her forward asking to end her widowhood. Two minutes after I said he'd be in heaven, you two went running past."

"Oh. Well, she's damned hard to figure out. I never expected her to come ask, that's for sure."

"And who are we talking about?" Amy asked. "Couldn't be Magda could it? I saw her downtown when I was shopping, had her hair done, bought a pretty new Hawaiian pattern dress. I haven't seen her looking quite so content since she arrived."

Greg lowered his eyes. "Well, the wood's no problem. I can sell you some today. I have a couple cords stored. I can bring a load with me when I come tomorrow. Mattresses though, that's harder, they might have them in town somewhere, but yeah, I'm not sure where and if they'd have enough."

Brock tried not to grin and make his embarrassment worse. "Two even right now is all we need. Did you find everything for the kitchen, Amy?"

"Plates, bowls, silverware, glasses, coffee pot, pots, pans, a few baking pans, knives, and utensils. Enough for basics. The rest I can pick up later. I need a pressure cooker. I think most of the nastiness was Mrs. Heinrichs rubbing it in. If we just keep our heads down, a couple days won't make things worse. If we're here most of the day it will help too."

Brock nodded, not liking leaving his family where people weren't happy with them being there. If his father started badmouthing them to Jane it could get bad quickly. It all came down to he wasn't there. And his own relations were the cause. Amy had... He'd just get angry again if he thought about it longer. "Then for now, how about Greg and I get started painting the rooms, and if you and BJ could go through the things we pulled out, see if they're usable or not. Stow what you can, but don't start putting things back until we've finished the inside. We aren't completely painting, so it shouldn't take us long. Whatever you see we don't have, make a list and maybe go in and start seeing if we can track it down. The mattresses especially. Oh, and the salvage place."

"Brock, are you expecting someone?" Greg asked.

"No." Turning around, it was Kelti coming walking over from his car. He didn't look happy as he got closer. "Can I help you?"

"You've been here all morning?"

"On and off. We took some trips downtown to buy supplies, the thing isn't quite livable. Can I ask you why us being here concerns you?"

Kelti put his hands behind his back, looking like he was at attention. "Sir, I'm sorry to tell you that your father is dead."

Brock stood up quickly. "What?"

"Not long ago, Thomas Harker and Jane Briggs were found killed down on the shore by the Cherry Blossom Inn."

"Killed?" Amy whispered.

"Yes sir, there's little doubt. They were both found with a bullet hole at the base of the skull. It rather looks like they were caught unawares."

Brock sank back on the bench in shock.

"You had some problems with the man, didn't you?"

He looked up quickly. "The gossips said that, did they? The same ones you're hiding being intelligence from. Were you here watching Jane by any chance?"

Kelti bit his pipe harder, and he knew it was true. "Sir, I'm not discussing..."

"I did not kill my father. I was disowned for years, I didn't just snap, and other than that house he had nothing. I, however, have about 15,000 dollars in the bank right now so that rather rules out money as a motive. If Mrs. Heinrichs is right I get nothing from him anyway. I have been here all day getting the boat ready so I didn't have to deal with Jane or my father. Wanting to do it before my father could turn Jane nasty against my wife."

Kelti look over at her interested. "They were killed last night by the look of it. About ten, not this morning."

Brock closed his eyes. "I was in the lodge with everyone else. I believe I was punching an ass of a private for attacking my wife about then."

"Can I ask what it was he did that has you so angry?"

"At this particular time, when this leave is over, my orders will send me back to war. I am not going to waste what time I have telling you why I didn't kill a bastard of a man when I surely thought about it. I've killed enough of the world and I have to live with it. But if all you have is wishing a man dead as reason enough, then go away. You're looking in the wrong place. We'll be right here should you find anything more that proves something we didn't do."

Kelti stared forever before men coming back to the boat works after lunch break broke the silence. The boat works there put out wooden mine sweepers that wouldn't set off magnet switches. They'd won 6 E awards for production excellence, the highest of any company. There were slim few others with 6 awards as well, but none higher. Bellingham on its own had raised enough money to donate a boat to the war effort. Some 600,000 dollars in nickels and dimes. Greg had talked about it the night before at dinner.

"Well I'll be damned Brock, when did you get to town?"

Brock looked close at the man. "Tommy Zaal. It's been a long time. Just got in two days ago, found out Harold left me his boat, and I need a place to live. It's just leave now, but my wife will need it regardless."

Tommy was a stocky man, red-faced and blond. He looked at Amy for a moment. "Well I'll be...you never said you'd married her. One lucky sod, I must say."

"Five years ago now, before I went off to China."

"Where's Harry then?"

"Died at Biffontaine last fall," Amy whispered.

"Oh, I am sorry," Tommy muttered, and finally Kelti wandered off looking downright ready to kill.

"Know anyone with mattresses we could buy?" Brock asked to change the subject.

Tommy stopped in thought. "I just might, now that you ask. Talk to Virginia; her family had the furniture store, but everyone could make far more working here. They still open it on Saturday for the extra money, but if you told her you needed it now I'm sure she'd meet you after she finishes up." He looked around and pointed to a group. "Virginia!" he yelled loudly and one broke off to come running.

"Brock!" She grabbed him in a big hug. She was a year ahead of him in school; they'd been in the school play together. "Is this your boat?"

"Harold left it to me, but we could really use some things for it. Mattresses mainly. We'd like to get out of the Inn."

"Of course. You know the parents' place, don't you? Come by, say, seven, and you can get whatever you need. Mattresses we have plenty. Oh, I have something you'll need, we got an order of cushions for something. No one quite knows what it was for, complete mistake, can't even track them. The company is baffled, frankly. I imagine they'd fit the built-in pieces here. Nice reddish ticking material."

"You want to come look quick to see if they'd even fit, no use pulling them out of storage if they won't work in the end."

"Sure." Virginia climbed around like she was a monkey and up in a second. By the time Brock got up she was measuring with her hands. "Oh they'll fit lovely, I think. There's not enough for the whole boat, but the dining banquettes, this big sofa-sized bench here. If you had a little time I could have Mrs. Hastings, our old seamstress, cover some other cushions that are similar size with a coordinating fabric for the other spaces. We have a real pretty red with dragonflies that would match, a small amount of a red diamond. Oh and a rusty-red-and-green plaid. There should be enough of those to make curtains for the dining room there."

Same old Virginia, running a mile a minute. "Yeah, there's time, I'm not expected back for a month, and Amy will be here until I can get back whenever this war ends."

Her smile died. "You aren't here for good?"

"Someone's putting in orders to possibly come stateside, but there's nothing definite. The request was for around here but that doesn't mean anything."

"Right, then we'll get you set up as quick as we can. See you at 7."

"Any idea about a pressure cooker?" Brock got out before she ran off.

"We had one but it was turned in for scrap with ma gone. She was the only one that knew how to use it. Haven't looked, to tell the truth."

"That's all right."

She ran off and Brock climbed out. "Greg, you want to get started on painting accents in the two largest berths? We have an errand to attend to. Could BJ stay with you? We won't be long if we could use your truck."

"Sure, just don't use up all the gas. I'm on my last rations."

iiii.

Brock pulled up to the lawyer's office and opened the truck door.

"What are we doing?" Amy whispered.

"We're going out to the house as soon as I ask one thing." He left before she could ask why the house. He hardly knew himself.

"Brock..." Mr. Meter started.

"Please, I don't have the heart to hear everyone ask when did you get back. I'm just on leave. I don't know anything more about the war than the rest of you."

"No, well then. What can I do for you?"

"Father's will. I just need to know if the gossip is true and he left it all to some organization. Oh, and Mrs. Heinrichs said something about signing some papers for Harold's boat."

"Like that old blighter will ever die. He's too damn stubborn," Meter snapped as he went over to a file and dug through it.

Brock took a deep breath. "He was found killed this morning out at the inn next door. I imagine the police will be keeping it quiet for now though. I'm sorry that I don't look properly grieved over the fact, but he cut me out long ago."

Mr. Meter stood up quickly shoving a table doing it. "Killed."

"I guess so, someone came to tell me not long ago."

67

He shook his head slowly as he took in the information. "I'm sorry Brock, but no, you were disowned completely. He left all his possessions to the something called Beta Theta Inc."

"Never even heard of it. Would you mind if I grabbed my personal things from the house then? They were still there while I was away."

"No, no, go get your things. I'm not a prison warden, just the executor. I'm guessing the beneficiaries will just empty it out. If you could sign these I can give you the papers for the boat."

"Thanks."

Brock sank back in the car, fuming. He knew he was disowned, it wasn't a surprise, but this was just ridiculous.

"What's wrong?" Amy asked quietly.

"The damned idiot gave it to some college fraternity it sounds like, they probably bought booze from him by the load full. But he said I could go in and take personal things."

She pulled back from him and stared. "We took those when we left."

"But he doesn't know that. Grab what you need for the boat, anything that might be useful while I'm riffling the papers. Oh and those Lummi carvings in my room, I want those. A friend carved them. I'm not going to have someone accuse me of murder because I'm convenient. We both know there's something going on."

Amy hid a smile as she looked out the window. "I should have known you wouldn't just tell the man to go away and ignore it."

"For all I know Kelti himself killed them and I'm just the fall guy."

"He wouldn't?"

"If Jane was stealing military papers and they saw her as a threat, it wouldn't surprise me."

4 gallons of gas didn't last long when making lots of trips back and forth that far out. Greg hadn't known he was coming back after all. Amy kept watching the needle get lower, leaning over to do it.

"Look in the garage. I think your father gets gasoline along with food. He doesn't make it to Seattle and Vancouver on rations," she said finally when they pulled into the drive of the house.

"Amy, you've been living here and working next door. What's out of place other than the black marketing?"

"Oh." She got out and headed to the house, deep in thought.

It didn't take long to find cans in the garage, hiding among the crab pots. He emptied a can into the tank for Greg and filled the back with another 10 along with all the crab pots and fish traps. He threw in the fishing rods and tackle too. Most of it was his anyway.

"I found a pressure cooker, we can put meat by when we do the summer in the islands. More if I can talk you into a grand tour. The charts are all there," Amy called when she heard him come in. Now she was talking around the world, and the war wasn't even over yet.

"I grabbed my crab pots."

"Should have guessed that's why you wanted the truck."

Brock looked slowly through each room, checking drawers and anywhere he could think of that might have papers or anything. He even checked the attics to little avail. Finally Brock sat down at the desk. His father wasn't the sort, it was a long shot that he would have something there, but still. Where else he would start he didn't know. Slowly he went through each drawer, most of it looked like he hadn't cleaned it out when his mother died almost a decade ago. He even checked the underside of the drawers. Turning around he started pulling some books from the shelves. Amy always needed something to read.

Damn. Brock rushed out of the room and up the stairs. The old hiding place during Prohibition, he should have thought of it first thing. There were several of them hidden among the ¾'s paneling. Pulling one hall panel among all that looked the same there was space to hold several cases of alcohol. There was still a case there even now. Good old Scotch from before the war. Brock took it out, but otherwise it was empty. There were three more cases to add to the first as he worked his way around to them all. Liquor runners road indeed. Amy watched him with care as he pulled another panel, rum this time, but as he took it out, there was a box on the side.

"Did you find everything we need?" Brock asked.

"Blankets, towels, the few things I was lacking for the kitchen. I pulled the food. I paid for most of it anyway. Any tin or container I could find. What medicines there were and first aid supplies. BJ gets himself hurt often. Those carvings you mentioned."

He didn't open it though. He really didn't want Kelti finding him there. "Then if we can get these out in the truck, let's get out of here."

Amy nodded and grabbed a case of alcohol. They just carried all out in a hurry.

"Well, look through it," Brock finally said when they were down the road.

"Oh." Amy opened the box slowly and gasped. Brock took a peek and there was cash, but more surprising, gold. Some coins as well as small bars.

"And you paid for most of the food?"

"Tom said that he hadn't any cash. He was barely getting by, he said." It wasn't the cash she pulled out though. A ring lay in her hand as she stared closely. "This was the ring stolen when the man apologized for getting me in trouble."

"What?"

She picked up a necklace with a rather nice ruby on it. "And this is the necklace that went missing just when I got here. That's how I thought I got the job, Tom said there were thefts and they needed a new maid to get it dealt with."

"What are the papers?"

There was silence most the way into Fairhaven before Amy looked up. "A letter must have been delivered to the wrong box. If we thought our letters were steamy then we have some lessons to learn." She fanned herself for a moment. "And it's from another woman. Loveliest Jane, from all my love Emily. I think this money and such is the blackmail from her over it. I don't think he stole it. When she was short she'd grab a few things and hand them over. He was a thieving ass, but there's nothing here that shows he had any other motives with the woman."

"Mrs. Heinrichs thought they were on pretty good terms for blackmail. I'd brought it up before."

Amy turned, staring at him. "You're right. They were rather chummy." Amy sat back in the seat, chewing on her fingernail, but then she turned the envelope over. "Oh well, that's another story."

"What?"

"Ever heard of Emily Vaughn?"

"No, why?"

Amy shook her head. "Sorry, it would have been after you left. She was caught in Boston when I was in school still. She was caught smuggling secrets to Russia. It was when the Soviets and the Nazis were on the same side still. The address on the envelope is a prison."

"Good Lord, if that's what's playing out here."

"I don't suppose you have an idea who killed them then?" Amy asked.

"Not a single clue. That just gives a motive, not a who. It could be, like I said, someone found her dangerous in our government and shut her up, or someone on the other side thought she was dangerous and shut her up. Assuming that Miss Vaughn is still in jail and not out for revenge for Jane falling for someone else."

Amy just laughed. "Brock, you're horrible."

"And what do you think someone would say about our letters if they were read?"

Her laugh died quickly. "Oh god, I hate to imagine."

"You're beautiful when you're blushing."

Amy stuck her tongue out, then she just froze. "Oh damn, there's a woman hiding at the Inn."

"What!"

"Jane had me delivering dinner to her the last week, but she'd shown up a month or so ago. She never said a name though."

Something was going on; what though was impossible to figure out.

The gas was down in the engine room, hidden from sight. Alcohol too. His father was getting to be more of an ass as the day went on. Amy slipped a key out of the office and opened the door to a cabin. The hidden woman's cabin. There was nothing left. It had been cleaned.

"She was here the day you arrived. I was here working before we came back and found you. I took her dinner," Amy muttered.

Brock looked around—nothing was left behind; it didn't look like it had ever been slept in. "So she either killed them or she ran when she heard about them dead. What on earth was going on?"

It took turpentine to clean off the varnish and paint on them before they made a visit to a furniture store. With all that being delivered the next day when Virginia went to work, they walked into dinner.

"Oh I am so sorry, Brock." Magda came running over and hugged him like they were long lost friends. That night, she wore a modern version of a Greek or Roman style wrapped dress, leaving one shoulder bare. "I can't believe your father is dead. It was horrible finding the bodies." Damn she was an actress. He would believe her scared if he didn't know more than most.

"You did?"

"Yes, of course. I went for a walk down by the shore after I had breakfast and almost stumbled over them. I thought there might be something interesting washed up after the storm. I never imagined..."

"That's enough!" Kelti called.

"And he's been strutting around here like he is in charge of the place," Magda whispered.

"He's intelligence." Brock muttered as he held out chairs for her and Amy. "When he realizes I didn't do it, the rest of you are the prime suspects or the prime scapegoats for whoever did kill them."

Magda stared with her huge blue eyes as he sat across the table. "What are you saying?"

Brock just shook his head.

"I have to see this boat of yours tomorrow, it sounds delightful," she said suddenly.

"If you do that we'll put you to work. It's not finished yet, it took us forever cleaning up to look presentable to come in tonight," Amy announced.

"Lovely. I've been getting bored here lately. I was told there would be more happening. And don't you dare tell me to go find the opium dens."

Brock hid a grin. "Oh they're all closed down now. Just brothels left for your fun now."

"Are there really?" Mr. Poole asked, almost falling out of his chair.

"I'm surprised you didn't know all those extra women that came after dinner last night..." Brock grinned to finish the sentence.

"Are you serious? And I never knew." Poole just gaped.

Brock just ignored him as Mrs. Heinrichs brought out dinner. Salmon with mustard sauce, buttered fresh asparagus, and a lemon cream pie. The woman was trying to get rid of it before anyone came and got her in trouble. No, she wasn't, other than a few things in the pie it was all local.

"He took all the alcohol, it's a dry house now," she whispered in his ear. "Can I bring the extra food to the boat before he comes looking in my kitchen?"

There it was, she was hiding it had ever happened, knowing there would be people roaming about looking for murderers. "Sure, if we can't use it there's somewhere we can give it away. Bring Magda to the boat when you do, she asked to see it."

"Thank you." She rushed off before anyone noticed her lurking.

"There's talk the Inn will close soon. Mrs. Heinrichs says there's no will to find. She's been trying all day. Then again we could just stay for free if there's no one to kick us out," Magda said, hiding her talking with a forkful. "Why is Kelti staring at you like he is?"

"He came around this morning to tell me about my father and then proceeded to all but say I had killed him. I kicked the man out, frankly."

Magda laughed faintly. "No wonder he came back in such a horrid mood. What is it with them, they hardly ever said a word before and now they've taken over."

"Kelti's never had a field job before so he's about as subtle as a tank. Charlotte is from New Orleans and scared to death someone will find out about her past. She was hired especially because she could chat up men.

"She's the more senior of the two with experience outside the office, but privates don't attract notice," Amy muttered under her breath.

"What do you mean chat up men, afraid someone will find out?" Brock asked.

"I think Charlotte was a prostitute before the war," Amy said quietly.

"What?" He and Magda both choked.

"You should watch what you say in front of a maid without realizing someone is there."

"Maid?" Magda said before she took a sip. "Oh lord you're her, the one Jane was having a fit over. I needed another towel yesterday and she came all but screaming you had quit. In that dress last night I never..."

"Looked at the maid."

"Oh I looked, couldn't figure out why such a woman as you was scrubbing toilets in this dump. It just never occurred to me that you'd go from maid to guest. Jane was just never letting up about a maid that ran off when her husband came home. I suppose she didn't want to tell me that I would be eating with her maid."

"They said that she was such a thing without noticing you were there?" Brock laughed.

Amy just smiled serenely. "No, they didn't know the kitchen can overhear everything in the dining room. They were out here alone when I was baking."

"You can?" Magda looked horrified. "You know who I was here seeing?" Magda hissed. If she could hear, then Jane could hear. An almost empty hotel, who wouldn't think of doing business right where they sat? Jane could overhear even just a snippet and then go riffle likely rooms. That was too left to chance though. Bellingham wasn't a great city, that men knowing things came and went often. A liberty town yes, but that was lowly sailors and airmen. They wouldn't know anything, and that wasn't the crowd that would have gone to an out-of-the-way inn. It was a war, stealing papers had to be the point, but this wasn't the place to get much of anything.

She didn't say anything more as Roy came over. "I haven't seen much of you since the other night," Roy asked.

Brock shook his head. "No, I found out someone left me a boat, we're getting it set up to live in instead of here. We were there when we were told about the murder."

"I wanted to ask about Europe. I never meant anything when we spoke before."

"Have a seat then." Brock reached for a glass and knocked it over on purpose. It spilled right in his lap. He went to the kitchen immediately as Amy cleaned up water. It was a habit hard to break it seemed, going from maid to guest in a day.

"Oh, look at you," Mrs. Heinrichs fussed.

Then BJ stuck his head in. "Are you all right?"

"Can you run back to the cabin and grab me another pair of pants?" He said it loud enough so the dining room would hear. Amy would have to figure out he wanted to talk to the woman and make sure no one came over. Just a nod before he was gone. "Mrs. Heinrichs, Linda, you know Jane was spying, don't you? You know everything around here."

She nodded slowly. "She said she'd call the police on me if I ever told when I found out, said she could make it look like it was all my doing. All because my grandparents were German, they'd buy it without question. Didn't matter to her I lost my husband fighting them in the first war and now my son in the second."

"Was she meeting someone?"

"She never told me things like that."

"Did you know she was in love with a woman?"

The old woman spun around, shocked, she shook her head a moment. "I know she has a man, not sure who it was. She could be a crude old bitch, she'd vanish for hours and then come back talking like she was...well, my mother would have slapped my face if I ever talked like that. Cocks and all sorts of talk, but not women. Why would you say that?"

"I found a letter at father's house addressed to her and from a woman."

Mrs. Heinrichs shook her head. "I don't know what that letter means, but no, she's not a sapphist. I'm pretty sure I've heard her mention as many as 4 children. All grown, they're serving in the war effort just about all of them that I know. She didn't like to talk to me about her private life though."

"Then what happened last night?"

"Tom was supposed to be delivering more stuff we didn't need. Smitty's not come back and I've been looking because of the cleanup. I don't know where he is. I told Kelti he was missing and no one seems to care. Me, I go to bed like I'm told and I don't get involved. I'd have left a long time ago, but I don't have a pension to live on, and who hires a 60-year-old woman?"

The door suddenly flew open. "Brock, heavens, it's just some water." Amy said loudly.

"BJ should be back with some dry pants for me any moment. Kelti's getting suspicious?"

She just nodded.

"Mrs. Heinrichs, do you know anything that could help?" Brock whispered.

"I found some papers a while ago, but I couldn't make heads or tails of it. Lots of numbers mostly."

"Kelti hasn't found them?"

"No. He hasn't looked at all that I've seen."

BJ came running in finally and Brock changed quickly. "After dinner could we look at them?"

"Yes, of course."

His dinner wasn't even cold when he got back. But Kelti glared. "What did you want to know, Mr. Carlson?"

"Call me Roy, please."

Before he could answer, Greenly made some very loud joke and the both of them were laughing hilariously.

"Is he here often?" Roy asked. "He seems to have made himself at home."

"Yes, he's here far more often than I like," Amy muttered. "Tried making me his wife a couple times."

"I don't blame him any." Brock winked.

"Wouldn't he have to get leave?" Roy asked.

Brock looked over slowly. "He should, it's Sunday night. I would think he had to get back even if he had a 48-hour pass. And if he's here that often I never got that much leave. I don't suppose you know where he worked before you said he was exiled here?"

Amy shook her head for a moment. "Oh yes, some little place called Hanford, WA. At least that's what one of his wives mentioned getting back to work there."

"Never heard of it," Brock muttered.

Roy nodded. "I went there once when I was a kid, tiny little place down on the Columbia River. I suppose there's some facility there now with the war. They seem to be everywhere."

"Probably."

"I'm no expert of course, but I imagine it's one of us in the room," Magda said out of the blue.

"Even you?" Brock asked.

Eyelashes lowered, she looked at him with quite a look of determination. Hard determination. "They wouldn't have been the first, but I had nothing against them."

"Two people are dead, and a third is missing. Someone had something against them."

"Who's missing?" Roy asked.

"Smitty. Mrs. Heinrichs hasn't seen him since last night," Brock answered.

"Try out at the Lummi Reservation where he's from, he's been seeing a girl. She's a baker at one of the hotels in town. If he isn't there, or she doesn't know, then he's missing. He vanishes all the time. Mrs. Heinrichs spends all her time in the kitchen, hardly notices unless he doesn't show up for the chores at about 10."

"Ask the maid," Brock muttered. But looking around, it was impossible to look at one of them and say they were a spy. Assuming that's what a single letter meant. A communist spy. Germans were the ones that everyone worried about; Russia, after all, was an ally. One no one seemed to trust. On that coast, Japan would have been a better bet even, it would have been sympathizers at that point though, internments made it impossible for nationals to roam freely really until they finally started letting them out.

"Were you at the bombing of Dresden?" Roy asked, getting back to his question.

Brock looked over slowly. "Is that what you want to know, if I helped bomb a city that might have had little value? Or are you just trying to piss me off as much as Kelti is, accusing me of murdering my father when I have to live knowing I've killed thousands if not tens of thousands?"

"Were you there?" he asked again.

"No, I'd been shot down bombing Berlin and had to bail out a week or so before they flew those missions. One of the new jet fighters. I kept it in the air long enough that, fortunate for me, the allies had recaptured the countryside I landed in. Is that what you wanted to know?"

"My own country is not free from them and you worry that a town was bombed. Yes some innocent people might have died, how many have they killed? I am not in the mood for this talk. I'd rather you ate somewhere else," Magda said it with little mercy in her voice. Magda just stared when he opened his mouth to answer. Finally he took his plate and went back to his own table.

vii.

Brock lay on the bed getting BJ to calm down and sleep, when the door swung open. He was just about asleep himself, to tell the truth.

"Oh sorry. You said you wanted to see these," Mrs. Heinrichs whispered.

"Can you make heads or tails of it, Amy?" He really didn't want to get up. Mental exhaustion or physical, either way he needed sleep. Closing his eyes again, there was just a faint hum of conversation between Amy and Mrs. Heinrichs. Faintly he heard Amy tell her to go get some sleep and they would see her at the boat in the morning.

"We should make a run to the reservation. If you two know things, Smitty must too," Brock murmured, hardly awake.

"Get some sleep, it can all be done tomorrow."

CHAPTER 5

Amy slipped out of the cabin and immediately felt watched. She always felt watched, how could she not, she ran from Intelligence. She was a slave there, unwilling to take BJ's only parent from him, she thought, by turning herself in or getting caught. Everything had changed when Brock sat there in a chair. Her heart was whole again. Now if she could just bring Brock's back, he said he wasn't the man that left her. It didn't take long to see that. The more he found out about his father, the more it ate away at him, and that didn't count the war. She knew there was nothing to find in Jane's office. She was pretty sure Tom had told Jane about her situation when she showed up for work; Jane treated her like a damn slave. Jane knew there wasn't another option. She was trapped there. The question was what did Jane know. Enough Jane never let on to more than black marketing. If Emily Vaughn was somehow involved, there was far more in this than stolen sugar. Brock was right, Tom wasn't doing it to be kind; ever since he said it, she knew, but why? It would all fall around him the minute Brock returned, or was that the problem? Tom never expected him to come back there, at least not until the war was over. He was kicked out.

Amy pulled out the phone over in Tom's house, fearful that someone would hear, and waited for the operator. "Long distance call to Arlington, Virginia, Cypress 980."

It took forever, it felt like, before there was finally a ring.

"Hello," came a far-too-groggy voice.

"General Maxwell, it's Amy."

"And you couldn't call when it was a decent time of day. Wait, Amy. What happened to you? We got the word that it was taking longer with your grandparents and then you dropped off the face of the earth."

"I don't know if anyone ever came around talking to you."

"No, why? You know you shouldn't be telling anyone about what you do, if they had I'd be worried."

"My husband just called to find out I wasn't in trouble, a neighbor called and turned me in when I got here. He turned me in for spying. I hid, I admit it."

"Wait, what are you talking about?"

"I speak fluent Japanese because my father was Japanese. My birth name is Amaya Kobayashi, my mother was a white farm girl."

"You called to tell me you lied?"

"I never lied. I married in 1940 to the now Colonel Brock Harker. Amy was the name I used since I was tiny. I'm as unJapanese as you can get. The only time I ever even ate the old foods was with my grandparents, my father loved hamburgers and ice cream and he married a woman that cooked them well. I never told a lie about it. My husband was in China fighting the Japanese when you recruited me."

"You never talked much of him."

"I thought he was dead, I just found out a couple days ago he's not, and he called to find out I'm not being hunted down. I hadn't dared to find out, worried even asking would get me hung for treason."

He laughed. "Amy, I knew the Japanese part. I never knew you had anyone investigating you. Do you think we gave you the clearance we did without knowing? Do you want your job back—I could use you?"

"Well at the moment my husband is only here for a month, until that's up or changes I'm not leaving him. I haven't seen him since he went to war. What I called for is I have a very large problem that I think you might be able to help me figure out."

"Now you're making me worry."

"You should be. Two people were killed here, one at least we suspect was a spy, possibly for the Communists. There was intelligence here for a week that we think was for her, but I can't come out and ask him. My husband says it entirely could be him that killed them to stop it, but the cook handed me some papers just now and it's big. I did tell him what I did, not fully though. He just knows I did code breaking but not where. I wanted to ask first before I told him more. The papers are almost identical to ones I worked on when I was at Aberdeen doing bomb calculations. Maybe more worrying is I found a coded message along with it. It's not our codes. I'd say it's Russian. Somehow an out-of-the-way innkeeper in Washington has them."

"Oh, hell. You're right that's worth a call."

"Is there anyone you know of working here, traveled through here, somehow she has them. We get a lot of military men coming through from Seattle." Suddenly something came through she heard a while ago. "Have you ever heard the name Greenly?"

"That pain in the ass..."

"Is he part of the Ballistic Research Laboratory?"

"No he wasn't at Aberdeen. I would have thrown him in the brig. His poor department head was pulling his hair out with the idiot. Top grades in his class, but when he got there he couldn't seem to keep his mind on anything but women. They pawned him off to some out-of-the-way post hoping he'd...it's where you are, isn't it?"

"Yeah, he's doing the same here. Seems to be getting his old women to come here and play wife for a week or so. Not to mention it is a liberty town, there are brothels all over the place. He's getting it wrong too, what I saw it was all messed up. They were missing pages, that's all that saved whoever losing all of it."

"Shit."

"What am I supposed to do, I can't tell anyone about what I found or I've committed treason. There's someone here that murdered two people, and for all I know he's still sitting at the Inn watching me even now. No one's left since then, so it's a good bet they're playing it cool."

"The easy part first, I'll put your husband in charge of the damn airfield, the man in charge obviously can't follow orders;

he was supposed to keep Greenly on track and if not, tell someone. It's been 6 months since he got there. All his boss got was it was taking longer than thought, and he was telling me it was taking longer than thought so it was never reassigned. That idiot is getting drafted."

"He's a civilian?"

"Oh yes, he was in college until a year ago, only took him 6 months to mess up where he was and get sent to where you are. Okay maybe I should ask is that husband of yours some paper pusher?"

"The last time I saw him was before Pearl when he went to China to fly with Chennault in the Flying Tigers, he's an Ace there. Right now he's with the 8th Air Force, he flew his 85th mission before he came here for leave. He was with the 2nd as well before Doolittle stole him. He's been in North Africa, Italy, England. I'm surprised he didn't want a divorce frankly, his family sent me word he was dead, I stopped writing in 1942."

"I'm more surprised that you didn't marry again."

"He's a hard man to follow, and you paid me enough I didn't have to settle just to have someone take care of me."

He just laughed. "No, long before I ever met you personally I knew you didn't need anyone to take care of you. Too many came back from giving you projects with tales of you putting them in their place when they tried picking you up."

"Yes their wedding rings made them fine upstanding men that I could see as a father to my boy long-term. I already had one child without a father."

Maxwell choked faintly. "You are absolutely right."

"What the hell am I supposed to do? We have a dead woman who may or may not be a spy and a dead black market smuggler that was my husband's father to worry about. Yes, she is dead, but if our intelligence didn't kill her then you have a Soviet most likely contact that could have collected who knew what before he killed her. We've found the name Emily Vaughn. What I was just shown I can't say if it was waiting for collection, had been sent already. I really don't want to get arrested if I walk up to the man here and say what we know, he's already accused Brock of murdering his father because of issues that he doesn't know, he just heard Brock had fought with him. We can hardly explain because to most a Japanese father makes me a traitor. Explaining makes it worse, he was thrown out over marrying me. But he was beating up a man that tried to attack me in front of an entire room when it happened. If the doctor was wrong and it happened after we went to bed..."

"Stop."

"General Maxwell, he dreams of falling endlessly after his plane runs out of gas because he's bombed the entire world into oblivion. Brock is here on leave, and they still make him fly local runs. Detached Service they call it. And if the war ends in Europe he's making sure I'm taken care of if he has to go bomb Japan. I'm not talking about some romantic notion that he had his arms around me all night, he wakes screaming. There's no missing a couple times a night, I don't even think he knows he does it that much."

"You'll have orders tomorrow he'll take command of the local field, I don't suppose you think he could figure it out?"

"He might. What do you have in that head of yours?"

"More than you probably think. Tell me why he might."

"He knows everyone, he grew up being trained to be the next in a family of smugglers and rum runners, he can fly and sail, he knows the area like the back of his hand and the people that aren't as upstanding. He wouldn't spend a lot of time asking the wrong people."

"And behind the scenes you'd know the right things if it was found. I wouldn't tell anyone you called, I think I'm going to make this agent rather angry." The phone went dead.

Damn. That wasn't why she called. She wanted to get this mess off Brock's hands, not saddle him with it. Amy stepped out into the night and let out a growl. Man never did really listen. She just didn't want to end up in jail. She wanted Brock unencumbered so he could sleep.

"What are you doing out here?" Charlotte asked out of the dark, and she jumped.

"Taking a walk. Is that a crime?"

"I stopped by your room and your husband didn't know where you were."

"Let him damn well sleep! Give me the boat any day. Even if there's no space at least we can have some privacy."

She walked past her and into the mist. Jane had built a covered seating area. Amy sank in a seat. Not that she could see anything. "Go away," she said in the silence.

"You shouldn't be out here alone."

"That is usually a requirement of being alone. No one else around."

"There you are," Magda called suddenly. "I found a missed bottle." She pulled up short when she saw Charlotte. "Oh. Well I don't have a glass for you, you'll just have to use the bottle." Magda sank down next to her and sloshed some rum in a glass before she handed it over. "My dear how do you ever concentrate on anything but getting that husband of yours in bed? Heavens, he is one gorgeous man. He must fuck like..."

"Trust me, he does." It was Charlotte that said it.

Amy spun around staring at the woman over her shoulder. They had showed no sign of knowing Brock when they arrived, the only option was the little idiot was out watching at the house. They hadn't even had a chance to do anything but sleep since they got to the Inn. "Get the hell out of here."

Charlotte just grinned.

Amy turned on a dime and belted the woman. Charlotte fell to the ground and sat there gaping, she scooted back when Amy came closer. "If I ever find you out in the dark watching like some damned pervert I'll do more than deck you. That husband of mine made sure I'm not waiting for him to come save the day when some idiot can't take no for an answer. Last night was shock he tried in front of a room, not that I can't handle him. Brock knew he wouldn't always be there like last night. I don't fight like some whore in New Orleans so get the hell out of here."

"You know?" Charlotte whispered.

"You want to learn about people, stop hiding in the dark and be the maid when no one imagines you're a human being that could listen, and certainly don't mention whoring while the maid is standing a foot from you serving asparagus loaf and beef stroganoff. I know more of what went on here than you can imagine, but no one's asked. No one's asked the cook, or the handyman, all I've seen you do so far is accuse my husband and confiscate alcohol. Didn't even seem to care that Smitty has been missing since last night. That won't find you a murderer, or do you not care because you killed them?"

Charlotte put a hand over her mouth. She looked like a little girl caught stealing a cookie. "That isn't why we were here. We aren't that sort of agents."

"It doesn't sound like you're doing anything to solve a murder."

"We aren't."

"No, then what kind of agents are you, watching the neighbors' house when a man comes back from war agents?"

"I didn't know anyone knew we weren't Northwest Sea Frontier."

"I'm not stupid. Northwest Sea Frontier disbanded last year, has another name now. You might call yourself Private and Lieutenant but dear, if you're going to do that, you wear rank insignia, not that US pin."

"I can't say why we're here."

"Then stop playing like you're in charge and confiscating alcohol like it means anything. Do your damn job and if you say spying on me in bed is part of that I'll hit you again."

"I just happened to be out and was near there, I swear."

"Then leave me the hell alone," Amy hissed.

"Yes, ma'am." Charlotte jumped up and ran.

Magda handed her the bottle as she sat down. "Now you know."

Amy narrowed her eyes. "You knew she...what is this place—spy central?"

"I keep my eyes open is all. You heard her talking about her past, I heard her talking about your performance the other night. You're ahead of me though, I didn't know she was here for something else. I suppose living in London means I don't know what all happens here to see that."

A swig of rum burned its way down. "You mean like you're here for something else?" Amy left her there.

ii.

Brock woke with a start, Amy caressed his forehead before he could even contemplate what caused it.

"I do it more than I think, don't I?"

"A couple times a night. I'm sorry, Brock."

He pulled her down to him. "Why are you sorry? You didn't start the war."

She rested her forehead on his. "No."

"What then?" he said with a great sigh.

"I kind of belted Charlotte. She was hanging around outside Tom's house the other night, the night you arrived. Said she'd heard us and I got pissed."

Brock started laughing. "I would have liked to see that."

"Can you laugh that I might have made things worse for you?"

"How is that?"

Amy kissed him gently. "I knew what Mrs. Heinrichs handed me, I called last night instead of telling you immediately. If no one was tracking me down I had to get permission, I was not some little secretary top secret unit. I was part of Arlington Hall, the code breakers. The ones breaking the whole show. There were two things in what she handed me. One is like what I did at the very start of the war, bomb calculations for something. Not all the pages were there to know exactly. The other was more serious, I do the Japanese codes, but it's in the same section as the Russian codes. Yeah, we don't trust them. There were a couple code messages I recognized. I can't figure them out, but I know what they look like. The part I'm sorry about is I think you'll have command of the airfield today. Top secret, Greenly kept saying, it popped in my head talking to him, and what I saw was top secret even if there weren't codes. General Maxwell at least knows who Greenly is, and the work he's supposed to be doing isn't getting done. You'll have to deal with the fact that Greenly was working on something and it's not finished, and the man that was supposed to keep him on task failed, and I think he rather expects you to figure out who killed them. And I'm supposed to help you find who the hell has codes to steal here in Washington State. Someone's stealing far more than should be here to even see. They don't leave the buildings."

He always knew she was a genius, there was never more proof than right now though. "Why didn't you say? Don't tell me I don't have clearance either."

Amy shook her head slowly. "I called just to get it off your hands. I figured if I told him security was breached then he would see it dealt with and keep us out of it. No one's supposed to know we can break Japanese codes or the British can read many of the German codes as fast as they can. You're on leave, I didn't expect him throw it on you. I was hiding for a very big reason, if I'm thought a turncoat it's serious. I have serious information I had access to. I figured it would be less chance of my being arrested than going and telling Kelti. Whatever Kelti's here for, the murder doesn't have to do with it. When I was yelling at Charlotte she let that much slip at least, but I don't know what they are doing here. They aren't trying to solve it. General Maxwell said not to tell anyone I called him though so I... "

"Should have hit her sooner, then I'd have spent more time trying to figure it out than working on the boat. What, he just postured a bit to make it look like he was involved to throw off why he was really here?" He sat up quickly, taking her with him. "Then what the hell were they doing outside the house before anything happened?" He started putting on his clothes in silence. The smile started as he put on his shoes. "There are only cliffs right here; if they were meeting someone, bringing something ashore, that's the only beach along here. The night I arrived was high tide, it would have been low by the time the shipment came in."

"You're going to tell me that there just happens to be intelligence here for several days without any connection to murders and spying going on in the same place."

He shook his head with a grin. "Since we haven't told them what we know, and they aren't talking with what they know, it's very likely they are related. But until there's something official here giving me a reason to look into all this I guess it's time to get some work done on a boat we own."

"Come on BJ, time to get up, its 8." Amy shook him gently and he groaned. "We have to go work on the boat."

He hopped up in an instant. "Now?"

"Only if you aren't in your pajamas."

He looked down and grinned. "Oh." He rushed over and started getting clothes. "What was the name of your plane? They say all the pilots have their planes named."

Brock actually felt his face warm. "Oh."

"What did you name it?" Amy whispered. It wasn't his imagination then that he blushed.

"It's called the Terror from the West. The gunner named it because the original crew was all from the West Coast."

BJ shook his head. "I like Night Rain better." He pulled on his shirt.

"Why on earth are you of all people blushing? Terror of the West isn't bad."

"You think a man wants to explain to his three-year-old why there's a painting of his mother in nothing but her birthday suit and a robe falling off her on the side of his plane? They saw my drawings I did of you. They'd named it but I was informed I had to put it up there while we waited. You're famous among horny airmen."

Amy put her hand over her mouth, and then he heard the giggle. "You haven't had the same plane for 85 missions, have you?" she finally asked.

"Well it's had two tails, three wings, 4 noses, and a new fuselage, but yes, the same plane."

"You're joking with me now."

"Considering I've been moving across divisions, yes. It's about my fourth plane. They've all had you on the nose though. I always had you with me. I always hoped I'd find you again, at least long enough to find you were done with me."

"Never." Amy pulled him close and kissed him. It never ended, not until BJ dragged them off.

iii.

"Aren't you sleepy heads?" Mrs. Heinrichs asked before they had even had a chance to set anything down. The boat was already in the water even in their lounging. Tommy must have gotten it done before they started work.

Greg was already there painting too, but that was superficial. They could be living there by night fall. Not that it was imperative anymore with Jane gone.

"You have a full load of wood for the stove," Greg called.

"Thanks."

Even more surprising, Magda stood there in work clothes,

not just there to lounge. "Well what do you need done?"

Amy looked around. "Greg, are the berths we did yesterday dry yet?"

"Yes."

"Then get mattresses into those two and the beds made. Unpack the clothes into the cupboard. That would allow us to sleep here. Then we can finish up getting things put away at out leisure."

"I have to get back," Mrs. Heinrichs announced. "We unloaded the food for you."

She didn't need to say it, things were lying around everywhere, making it hard to walk. How much fell off a ship, this was ridiculous. "Thanks. Amy, how about you go through it all and fill what we can use here, and then if we can borrow your truck again, Greg, we'll take it out there so we can walk. You can grab what you can use. We'll distribute the rest when I make a run later."

"If there's coffee, I'll take a pound. I'm a bachelor though, I eat at the café most of the time."

Brock dug around. "Done."

"Hand me two of those before you take that box out." Amy said. "How about we see what's in them now and take them out as we look. I can hardly move."

Brock just nodded and soon they were calling out things and pulling and carrying out. The entire back of the truck was full; the rationing board would have them locked up if they caught one look at it. They covered it all with a tarp.

Brock stared right at Magda. "Do you have anything you wanted to say without being heard in volunteering for work?"

"You're looking into this, aren't you?" Magda whispered. "You don't strike me as the type to just let it go."

"I'm not letting myself be accused of something when I didn't do it. The man was my father, bastard that he was. I at least want to know who killed him even if I'm not terribly surprised it happened."

Magda went and closed the door, shutting Greg and Amy inside. "I'm worried now that I've heard what I have that I'm the reason."

"Your guest that was here?"

She nodded slowly. "He sent all his money ahead when

he saw how the winds were blowing in 1939, he's Czech, and three months later the Germans came in. He knew something would happen, just not when, and he was caught. Later he was sent to Treblinka, helped build it actually. He was one of the very few that escaped when the camp was to be finished, most didn't make it. I helped him escape Europe some time later and he came here. He knows I can get money in to help free our country from the Soviets or help rebuild it, but he will not go back. He is too sick to survive it long, no family left so he wants the money to help his country. But I don't know why here, why would we come here of all places when the bits I've heard make it sound the worst place we could have chosen. Your wife said anyone in the kitchen could hear?"

Brock narrowed his eyes. "I don't see how it would be you. Did anyone know who he was? Did he get away safe?"

"No and yes, but..."

"Neither of you carried anything that could have been looked at or stolen?"

Magda shook her head. "No he was very careful that no one knew he met with me."

"Germany is defeated whether the surrender has happened yet or not; you don't need to hide here."

She leaned near him, and he could see Amy inside, realizing they hadn't come in. "My father went back with the money following the liberating troops," she whispered. "If the Soviets get to Prague first and they find out he has it, allies or not, I don't trust them. The last word out I received was the Resistance had started rising up a day or so ago and now nothing. 'Prague is in great danger. The Germans are attacking with tanks and planes. We are calling urgently for our allies to help. Send immediately tanks and aircraft. Help us defend Prague. At present we are broadcasting from the broadcasting station, and outside there is a battle raging.'"

"You said your father is part of the government in exile?"

"I lied a little. He was once, but the Czech leader Beneš thinks the Soviets will give us a better chance and father doesn't agree. He's left them, now he's preparing for if the Communists get control. If it's all his paranoia he'll give the money he's raised to them, but..."

"If news gets out..." After what was happening in Russia

itself no one could say it was unfounded. "I wish I could say I knew more, how long ago was this?"

"Ten days ago."

"And you said something that could cause trouble perhaps overheard?"

"I don't think so, most of the time we were down on the beach when we were talking. I just don't know about little things we didn't think about, it wouldn't have been the major pieces. I just don't know. The minute I stumbled on the bodies and saw they weren't an accident, all I could worry about is if someone coming for me found them."

"Come on, let's go inside." Brock walked in and sank on a bench. "Amaya?"

Using her full name made her turn from putting some curtains up. "Are you telling everyone?"

"I'm telling you, it's up to her to tell Greg. This is Princess Magda Starek. The woman using opium and sleeping with warlords was her long-dead sister. She's in the Resistance, helping Czechoslovakia. Her husband was a prisoner of war and died, she has a son living in Britain. One of her husband's cousins flies with me, when someone doesn't say they are a princess I kind of guessed I should keep my mouth shut. Did you hear anything at all when her guest was here? We have the name of a spy connected in this, if Jane heard anything and it was sold or passed on like we think, it could ruin things Magda has in place."

Amy sank down on a seat. "What, you thought you were being funny last night?"

Magda shook her head. "No, never funny. I was keeping my eyes open, there had been a murder and I saw her following you. I never thought she would be stupid enough to say what she did."

"Is that true?" Greg said suddenly from the other room.

It didn't faze Magda. "Yes."

"Well that explains why I couldn't figure you out. You didn't fuck like you slept around."

Her eyes snapped over to him, she was pissed. Standing nose to nose with him, there was no missing it. "You're the second man ever. I've been a bloody widow since '43, he worried about me running off and he was the one that died. I'd hardly seen him since Czechoslovakia was overrun. He was shot down in '41. My son hardly knows me, because he was over near Greece and I couldn't get to him. They had to slip away on a boat to Cairo because most of the island died. I don't fuck."

Greg's gentle hand pulled a strand of hair from her cheek. "That was exactly the point. There was so much more in your eyes than the woman at dinner talking of brothels and drug dens."

"Brock said something of Magdalena had to survive the war and the woman without all the stories and games to stay safe wanted you."

"Amy, before they start having at it in front of us did you hear anything at all?" Brock said quietly.

Magda started smiling. "He's very good. I'm sure you'd enjoy the show."

"Yes and so would BJ standing there at the door."

Greg looked rather sheepish. "Oh, right. Are you really a princess?"

"Yes, it was my husband's title, he was poor as dirt, and I'm living off the kindness of friends to keep up the façade, so no one sees the woman heading into a war zone, and Hollywood connections to keep me dressed while I play the part."

Greg started laughing. "I knew I had seen that dress before."

"Amy, when my guest was there did you hear us saying anything that might have been something we shouldn't have let out?" Magda whispered. "We did our business outside, but if we weren't thinking at meals."

"You called him once and he didn't answer. He used another name didn't he?"

Magda turned quickly away from Greg, "Oh, you clever woman, I was so worried when I saw them dead I completely forgot he had..." A second later she kissed Amy soundly on the cheek. "I know we never mentioned my father in the open. All it might take was knowing his name to possibly work out what we were doing."

"Are you going back?" Greg whispered.

"If the Soviets get there first I don't dare, that's nothing to do with my activities. I know what they do to any woman they find. My father is waiting for the country to finally get freed so he can see where things stand. If the US gets there first there's a chance it won't end up Communist. All I can do is wait."

"Can we get some place to live by any chance or are we just going to talk all day?" Brock asked.

"Only if she tells me how on earth she gets into Czechoslovakia. It's surrounded. France I could understand." Greg remarked.

Magda just grinned. "That, love, is a secret I can't tell quite yet, might still need it. Maybe you'll just have to marry me if it matters so much. I might tell a husband." She walked down to the berths, leaving him there staring.

iiii.

In an all-out effort they had the berths all finished. The water tank was full. They were moved in. Not that everything was there, but everything they had was prepared. Magda had a meal on the table. They had finished at last and sat there for a moment of rest.

"Colonel?" Magda said quietly.

Brock turned to look. Stephens did not look happy as he stormed up the gangplank. "What's wrong? I don't see how giving me a flight to take should make you look so dreadful."

"You've been given command of the Airfield." He shoved the orders in his hand.

"Why do you look ready to kill me?"

Stephens walked almost nose to nose. "I'm sent to Narsarsuaq Air Base -- today."

Well that was one thing he'd not have to deal with, the one that let Greenly get away with sitting there for 6 months without telling anyone. The question should be though, was Greenly that important? Everyone knew of his work, code breakers wouldn't know bomb trajectories. And if the calculations were so important, why were they put in the hands of a moron that couldn't do them in an out-of-the-way place. "Greenland."

"You know it? I had to look it up."

"It's one of the stopovers on the oversea route from Europe. I've been there a couple times. The last time was just a week ago."

"It's a dump!"

"It's bigger than here, there are some 4,000 stationed there. Thousands of planes go through there." It was all true, even if Stephens would hate it.

"I'm from Hawaii, my mother owns half of Kauai, I'm supposed to be the first governor of the state. What do I know about snow?"

Or serving. Hearing that, it was likely someone had pulled strings to keep him out of fighting. And then sent him black market goods to make it comfortable. "As much as I knew about North Africa or China or Italy, or England. You'll learn."

Stephens shoved a rather large packet at him and stomped off like a pouting boy.

"You aren't leaving, then?" Greg asked, taking a sip of coffee.

Brock opened the envelope and his new orders were on top. "I guess not, a two-year post or until the end of the war, whichever comes first." He leafed through the packet and tucked half of it under Amy's leg. "And it seems I'm in charge of the investigation of the murders, since government information was found. Looks like I'll be busy instead of on leave. Greg, you want to be a local liaison—I could use someone that knows his way around these parts. Most these airmen here know the field and the bars."

His face lit up. "Sure."

"You want to go find the sheriff and learn everything you can. Tell him a military connection came to light and we have an interest in the case now. Smitty should be out at the reservation. I need to go talk to him and take all that food out there. Good place to get rid of it, where it's needed and no jurisdiction."

Greg looked pale suddenly. "Brock, Smitty's dead. I heard about it when I went for dinner last night. I thought you knew. The caretaker found him washed up on the shore at Larrabee State Park late yesterday. He'd been shot, not like the others, but still shot, and he'd been there since the other murders, it wasn't fresh."

Brock wrote out a quick note. "Greg, I want official details now, not the café gossip. Go put your uniform on, and you're on temporary service. Don't take any crap. I'll be at the inn. If I'm not there, call the airfield and tell me when you have it. Take that food out there regardless."

"Yes, sir." Greg ran.

Brock made his way back to their berth and pulled his uniform out of the cupboard.

"Brock..." Amy whispered behind him. "I'm sorry. I thought he would send someone else to handle it, not you. That's the only reason I called instead of telling you first thing."

"Oh, you know me, I'm not subtle enough, it's probably better I have command of it, then I can't get in trouble doing it anyway." Brock pulled out a gun tucked in the closet. "Don't trust anyone. You remember how to use it."

"You're scaring me."

He took her face in his hands. "We should have been scared when it happened. I thought someone was at least trying to solve this, so I let it slide. Other than a missing hidden guest, no one's run off. That means they're dangerous if we find them out. I don't think anyone just passed by and killed them. It's someone at the Inn. The boat has a motor, I want you to take it to the yacht club in Chuckanut Bay. Put it to anchor and sit there. If it's not me, start shooting. I'll be there for dinner. I'll bring everything and you can help me figure out what's going on."

"You're going to make me..."

"Nothing happens to you or BJ. I couldn't stand it, not again. If they're after anyone that worked there, you and Mrs. Heinrichs aren't safe. There's a lookout post there, I heard, someone will be watching and with the yacht club there, the private boat won't look out of place like here."

Amy finally nodded.

"Wait here until we're gone." He kissed her gently and hated the look in her eyes as he left her there. "Magda, I don't suppose you could call this contact of yours and find out how he chose here. I have to know how big this is."

"Right now?"

"Right now, we've lost a day already."

The woman froze. "What am I missing?"

"I was given the orders to figure this mess out. There were photos of papers found that seem to be top secret, there seem to be some Russian codes found that are definitely worrying. We found a letter mentioning Emily Vaughn. Amy says she was in jail for treason. A communist spy. She sent a letter to Jane. We're worried if there's one spy..."

Magda grabbed her purse and was off the boat before he was. As Brock pulled away, he made sure he saw Amy pull up the mooring lines. They'd been tinkering with the engine the day before, making sure it ran. She just had to pull ahead into open water and get around some spits of land. A beginner could handle the 60-foot boat for that much, and she wasn't a beginner. She was a fine sailor after their summers.

He made a quick run to the airfield, and Sullivan ran out the moment he appeared.

"Sir, is it true? You're our new commander."

"Yes, my orders are right here. Take Miss Stárek into the office and let her use the phone."

"Why?"

"Just do as I order. If I see any more sneaking luxuries on board planes I'll see the lot of you stationed in Antarctica. Where does Greenly work?"

Sullivan narrowed his eyes but pointed to an office down the hall. "Name's on the door, but he keeps it locked."

Brock kicked the door in, it only took a couple strikes. The noise brought men from everywhere close. They all stared as he grabbed an old crate and started emptying the desk of anything he could find.

"Whoever isn't working right now I want all of you out to the Cherry Blossom Inn immediately. You aren't there to party, start searching everything. The main rooms, the out buildings, the grounds, the beach. I have evidence that the owner was involved with stealing information from guests, her military guests. I'm not looking for evidence of the murders. I want to know what the hell is going on at the Inn. No one leaves and you make sure the cook, Mrs. Heinrichs, is safe. There are two people alive that have some clue what was going on out there, they will be safe."

"Give me the maid to watch then she'll be safer than a

baby in its mother's arms."

"You talk about my wife like that again and you'll spend the rest of the war cleaning my toilet."

The men all stood at attention suddenly.

"Now get down there and start looking. Anyone tries to stop you, throw them in a room and lock the door until I get there. Miss Stárek needs a phone."

They all scattered. All but one. Kingfisher stood there.

"Yes?" Brock snapped, as he started pulling out the drawers even. There were some pages shoved behind, they looked to be him hiding that he messed up a lot. If Greenly was a genius then something was wrong.

"Greenly isn't here, sir."

"No, he's playing house with some girl down at the Inn still, put him on report immediately. Even if he had 48 hours, which I doubt, he's overdue." Which was odd in itself, murders at the Inn, and his 'wife' didn't seem to care.

"That was asking if he wasn't here. I wanted to make sure."

Brock looked up from Greenly's incompetence. "And what can't he overhear?"

"I'm the clerk. You'll want to see his file, sir."

"I know he's a civilian."

Kingfisher went out and connected the phone call for Magda before he returned. He handed over a file and stood at attention. Brock opened it to a hornet's nest. "Stephens mentioned he was from Hawaii."

"Yes sir, they're half-brothers. I heard from another clerk, the father donated a boat to the war effort to keep his sons here and out of the fighting."

"And he's 20. There's no way he graduated from college."

"No sir, he was in his first year when they heard he was to get drafted and his father fixed a place for him in one of the offices. Over-played his skill, and the ready supply of women...he pulled some strings to get him here under his brother's watch."

"Stephens is gone?"

"Yes sir. The plane was waiting to take him to his new post when he got back from informing you of your new post. Anything you need, just ask."

"I need to know what the hell has been going on here?"

"In what manner, sir?"

"There were papers of Greenly's found at the Inn among the owner's things."

Kingfisher froze in place. "He's too damned girl crazy...he sits in here cursing most the time."

"Somehow those papers got out of here and ended up there. That's why I'm assigned here today instead of my leave. Something serious is going on here, and I'm getting pissed! Hanford? What's in Hanford, Washington? I heard it mentioned one of his women is working there I think."

"I can find out for you, sir."

Kingfisher vanished again and Brock finished ripping apart the office. There was nothing left when he was done. Stepping in Stephens's office he started the same thing. He kept the airfield running well by the look of it. Planes sent off on time; other than his brother being allowed to get away with murder, he wasn't a bad administrator. If his brother hadn't been his downfall he probably would have been a good officer. A half-brother at that, and with a different name, an illegitimate brother most likely. Other than getting some luxuries sent now and then, he ran it well.

When Kingfisher returned he had the guards' log book. "Does this help at all, sir?" It was open to the last few months.

"Do you get many visitors?"

"Not ones that aren't military."

He still ran through the lines since Greenly arrived, 6 months there wasn't much to see in the list. "Kelti was here?"

"Yes, sir, he came a few days ago, before the murders."

"What did he want to see?"

"He just kind of wandered around, an inspection, he said. Didn't really talk to anyone, or come into the offices. He spent the whole time wandering out among the buildings."

More cover it sounded like. Or there was something else. "Show me where."

Kingfisher led him out to the other end of the base. They ended up very close to the water; the bay was only a few hundred yards in front of them. "He went all the way down to the water."

Brock nodded and cut his way through the trees and

brush. Across the water was the Lummi Reservation, between, it was more of a mud flat, really. With the tide out it looked much farther than it was to the actual shore. They were looking for a place to come ashore. It seemed like that was the only thing he could figure out here, and hanging out by the house to hear him and Amy. Kelti wasn't that oblivious, he wouldn't just wander around inspecting places that meant nothing. He was there for something. The sea frontier was an excuse. Amy said it had been disbanded the year before. But what? Heading back to the office, Magda waited for him.

"Let me make a call," Kingfisher said in the silence.

"You haven't asked who told him," Magda said quietly.

"Sorry, I have a lot on my mind."

"He said it was someone called Gerald Campbell."

Brock turned and let out a growl. "Your contact lives in California?"

"You know who Gerald is?"

"Harold Campbell was the neighbor for years, when he died he left it to his son, Gerald, and he sold it to Jane. The Cherry Blossom Inn was his house growing up. He didn't want to stay here though."

"So it's a dead end."

"A coincidence it seems. Gerald is certainly no communist. He'd gladly marry a princess if he could."

Magda let out a laugh. "Or since those are sparse on the ground other than me, a film star in Hollywood."

"Precisely." Which might be why his father had left his collection of Chinese goods to Brock instead of his son. He had to know it would be sold immediately.

Kingfisher walked in but he didn't speak out loud; he leaned near Brock's ear and said one word.

Brock looked over at him quickly. "Are you serious?"

He nodded. "If you want to get him in trouble, he's not big on keeping his mouth shut. If Greenly isn't lying to me, he says that they have all of it parsed out wherever they can. Half the college maths programs have been commandeered to do the work the government doesn't have the men to do it. He doesn't even know what he is working on. He walked in with a pile of papers he said were top secret and he had to have them done. Then he closed the door and I usually just heard cursing."

"Yes and if that horny boy is responsible for something so important, you tell me why no one cared it sat undone for 6 months. You're saying the end of the war is in Greenly's hands?"

Kingfisher stopped mid-typing. "Oh we're all in trouble then, sir."

Brock really had a bad feeling. "Magda, get in the car."

"What's wrong?" she whispered when they got down the road.

"What do you know about Petya?"

"It's his first time out of Russia. He's not your problem."

Brock stopped the car on the side of the road. "Too much is going on here for some town in Washington. I am not in the mood."

Magda shook her head. "Like I told your wife, I keep my eyes open, nothing more. I am on leave like you since my guest left. You called her Amaya."

"That is her name."

"She's not full Japanese?"

"Half, her mother is white. Smartest woman you'll ever meet and that's not me sticking up for my wife, she is. She's not a maid, it's a long story."

"Why do you ask about Petya?"

"Some codes were found among Jane's things. Amy says they're Russian. She can't read them though."

Magda turned; her blue eyes had seen so much. Too much like him. "How can you trust me with that information? National Security could be destroyed..."

"We have bigger problems than Amy being a code breaker. We can't break Russian codes even if you know so it doesn't really matter. She hasn't been there in months. I need to know what is going on. Now."

Slowly she looked back out the window. "I called about him when I got here. I had to trust him before my guest came."

"I thought you said it was only the two of you there then."

"Yes, I planned it in the end when Petya was on an inspection tour. No chances even though he is..." She laughed faintly. "I wouldn't risk him knowing my business, but he's on the edge of deserting. His name is Volodymyr

Kompanichenko, he jokes about going to the camp again, but he doesn't need to be sent there to suffer. He's a Ukrainian Cossack, they'll murder him in his bed, set fire to his village, wipe out every last bit of his blood, and that was before there was a war. Petya was a friend of his that died. There was a bombing, Petya died just after he was ordered to report to the US to facilitate these shipments for Lend Lease. Volodymyr picked up his papers and stepped on the plane. He's not going back, they'll know he's not Petya the moment he steps foot there, but for now he's paid and safe. He is a writer, two points against him—an intellectual Cossack. The codes very well could be his, I'm not saying that. But I very much doubt he's the one that killed an old man and woman. He will not do anything to hamper his walking off and hiding among the masses. If he vanishes then you'll know that he received orders to return home."

"How do you know that?"

Magda pulled out a cigarette and lit it, she made it sensual every time she did it. She knew she did. "Love, just because I hadn't slept with anyone but my husband doesn't mean I don't know the value of sex to get a woman what she wants. I keep my eyes open. We were here for days; if I didn't worry about my home becoming communist before, I do now after our talks. They're no better than Hitler if they want someone out of the way, and everyone is afraid of them. He's been promised sanctuary with a house a friend has. Off US soil with a new passport and name."

"The island where your son was."

"Smart man. There was a population of Russians there, aristocrats that fled Stalin when the revolution started. The Germans were not happy to find them there, they were among the first to die. It's all but decimated, they need people to rebuild, like all of Europe. He's been promised the name of one. A son that no one knew existed for a family that is dead. Nothing has been turned over though, and he'll never get it if I thought he was a murderer. Death at home, death here if I tell who he isn't, or a new life. I've got him over a barrel. If you find proof he did it that's one thing, but if the only proof is because he is a Soviet, those arguments won't hold up."

"And the rest?"

"Mr. Poole is a letch always staring at me or Amy when she was still working there. Roy only showed up recently, never really talked to him. Kelti's -- I'm not sure about him. He really doesn't talk much. They just sit there whispering to each other. Charlotte was the same, kept to herself. Neither of them really said much to anyone until the murder happened, then he had plenty to say. And Charlotte, I never would have imagined she'd say what she did to Amy. You showing up really got people talking, there wasn't much mixing among the guests before that. Everyone wants to hear of Europe, what with the end coming, hopefully."

"Hmmm."

v.

Pulling into the Inn, there was sun for once. Blue as could be, a hint of the summer to come. Greenly was screaming at one of the men searching his room.

Kelti came running. "What the hell is going on?"

Brock headed over to Greenly though ignoring him. Daisy cried on the porch. Brock handed him his draft papers and the yelling at his former friends faded.

"What do you mean I'm drafted, I work..."

"Get packed, you report tomorrow. And I wouldn't call your father. Stephens is reporting to Greenland. He can't help. Someone that knows their math has seen your work, and I guess it wasn't up to standards; since you aren't doing that you're drafted. But first get into the dining room. We're having a talk." Brock turned his back on him and, as he passed Kelti, only stopped briefly. "There's a third person dead while you have a bloody spy working here that you didn't even seem to know about. Stealing work that a damn kid over there has been mucking up, covered over by his brother not saying he's an idiot, while his father throws money around to keep them out of fighting. I don't care what you think your case involves, but if you think it's unconnected to all that's happening in front of your face, then you're far stupider than I gave you credit for. When I have talked to Greenly we are going to discuss this, and if I get anything less than full cooperation you won't be happy with me."

"So the orders I got saying I was your driver aren't a mistake." Kelti whispered.

Brock bit his lip before he started laughing. "My orders said I was to figure out what happened; if you don't wish to be my driver, I would suggest you tell me what the hell you're doing here." He left him there.

Inside, he took over a table and Mrs. Heinrichs brought out coffee immediately. "I'm sorry, but Smitty's dead."

"What?" She sank in a chair, looking like her legs would fail.

"He was found over on the shore of Larrabee last night. I'm guessing he was shot trying to get away the same night."

A tear ran down her cheek and she rushed off as Greenly appeared.

"Sir?"

"Papers of yours were found here in the hotel by Mrs. Heinrichs, not in your office."

"Here? The only time they ever left the office was weeks ago. A girl that came to visit, she's a computer and she was helping me with some pages. I still had them when I left. I don't know why anyone would steal them, I don't even know what they're for."

"Or how to do them?"

Greenly lowered his head. "No, sir. I didn't know when Father got me out of being drafted I'd end up in something like this. I'd have done better I think if he had just let it happen. At least then they would have taught me what to do, instead of just thrown into something so much over my head. We didn't have a clue what to do, how would we tell I didn't know anything without bringing up all of Father's bribes and such. He has them thinking I'm such a genius that I graduated college at 19. I thought if I messed up awfully I would get fired and save it being found out, but he pulled another string sending me here. Will my brother be safe?"

"He'll be cold, but fine. He should be lucky; they could have sent him to the brig for this mess. When you brought the papers with you, tell me who was here, what happened? Everything."

He didn't ask to sit, at least. He stood at attention in

silence for a moment as Kelti slipped in the back. Charlotte with him. Brock tried not to laugh when he saw the distinct black eye the woman sported.

"It was fairly empty, me and Janet, a Mr. Gates, a Colonel Pritchard on leave from Bremerton. There was a woman, what was her name? Her and Jane had a huge row, the only real entertainment that weekend. There weren't any parties. Amelia Richards, that's it, she was a Canadian. Just there for one night."

Brock looked up at the man. One night, no one got in flaming rows in one night, not with a stranger. "Did you discuss those pages that were found in public at all?"

"Well, no one ever said not to, we were talking about it over dinner. We had them out discussing them. Funny thing was I thought I've seen her around here since then."

"Where?"

"In town. The grocery store—must have been over a week ago. She didn't act like she knew me, we ate dinner at the same table even."

"Go get packed. You have a bus to catch to your induction center. Send Daisy home."

"Yes, sir."

"Were you at Hanford, Washington before?" Brock asked before he reached the door.

"No sir. I was in the DC area near my father. He put me in the middle of geniuses that really knew what they were doing. I'm given crap to do. No one has even asked if I finished it, I'm sure it was busy work. No one would incur my father's wrath, but they know I'm useless. One of my friends that came had transferred there since I came here, she never spoke of what she did. Does it matter?"

"No, I heard it mentioned is all. I've been overseas for a long time, don't know half of what is going on in my own state. You can go now." Brock took a sip of coffee and closed his eyes. "This is a complete and absolute guess, but are you trying to find a woman named Emily Vaughn." When Brock opened his eyes, Kelti and Charlotte were gaping.

"Yes, sir. She escaped from prison a few weeks ago, some of her mail seemed to come from here and go to here. We were sent to see if we could find her. It was thought since it was so close to Canada she'd try to get over the border here."

"And you've been looking to find a place she could get away on a shore somewhere? Instead of just hopping in a car and driving over the border."

"I never meant to hear anything, sir, I swear," Charlotte whispered.

Brock waved them closer so he didn't have to yell. "And it didn't occur to you when people were killed that it might be connected?"

"We looked but we never found any connection at all."

Brock dug in his pocket and pulled out the letter his father had held over her head. He just held it out. Charlotte quickly took it from his hand and scooted away. Probably worried she would get hit again.

"You learn your lesson with my wife?" Brock asked, and she turned red.

"Yes, sir. Never bring up sex again."

"Then you learned nothing, she seduced me, Private. It's nothing to do with her not talking about sex, she'll turn your ears red. You don't hang outside her window and then brag about it. And if you hadn't gone around making it seem like you were looking into the case someone might have been actually doing it. All the local police know is there are three dead people out here and you seem to be thwarting them finding out anything because of your posturing."

"Yes sir."

"You were looking too far afield. All that fine food you've been eating that my father smuggled here from some shipyard."

"He had a boat then?"

"Yes, they could have been negotiating getting Emily out that way. We found that letter with her name on it as well as gold and cash. I don't think Jane had that for some extra sugar and coffee. I have the men searching the hotel. I suggest you do the same with what you know and see if we can't figure out who killed them or what exactly Jane was doing with top-secret papers, that Greenly was far too lenient with their care."

"That's what that idiot was working on," Charlotte gasped. "That boy who was trying to pick me up while his wife has her back turned."

"Brock!" Greg came running in, out of breath.

"What on earth?"

"There's a woman found not far from Smitty. She hadn't been found yet when gossip hit the café last night. Here's the files."

"Emily's dead too. What on earth happened here?" Kelti said quietly.

"I gave you orders, the office is upstairs. Go start looking through it all," Brock ordered. How could he trust any of them really?

"Yes, sir."

They were gone before Greg sat next to him. "I dropped the food off. They were grateful, they'll use it for the funeral, sent you some smoked salmon as thanks when I said you were on a boat."

"They were looking for the woman you just mentioned. She escaped from prison. But that doesn't explain why they're dead though."

"No." Greg went quiet.

Brock stared into his coffee. If his father was preparing to take them onboard and sail them somewhere, or even just Emily, it was a good bet that he wasn't just making a run up to Vancouver. One of the islands would be a better guess. No news would get out to them quickly, certainly not about little things like treason and spying. If they had money, which handing out gold and cash seemed likely, go buy a little house somewhere. No one the wiser. What on earth had happened? That explained part, it didn't explain that papers had been stolen for some time. It wasn't a one-time deal with a mention of something intriguing heard over the table. Then what? Escaping to the islands didn't exactly fit with stealing new info. It didn't mean anything unless it was given on, sold on. The storm that came in though, that was a wrench in the works. Getting the goods on shore before it hit was doable, good cover even. But there wouldn't have been a trip to escape Emily being hunted. Emily wouldn't have left that way, not that night in the storm.

"Tell them something was stolen from your room that you never noticed with the murders and your men got carried away brown-nosing with the new commanding officer," Greg said quietly. "There have been tales of thefts here ever since I got back, not long, I know, but long enough."

"Go spread that around. Even better..." Brock dug in his pocket, he had the stolen items Amy had recognized with him, hoping he could track down the owners and return them. "We found these at Tom's house. They were stolen from here, Amy knew a couple of them. Say we found them in looking. I think Jane took them." Greg rushed off.

"How long have you been back?" Brock asked as he got to the door.

Greg looked over his shoulder. "Lost my arm in January, spent a couple months in the hospital. Just got here beginning of April, a month really. There were theft rumors even before I enlisted though."

Brock just nodded and Greg ran off.

No one heard a noise, so a silencer most likely. Either while the dancing was going on or in the night with a storm. It had to be earlier before the storm hit; they wouldn't have been out in the weather once it got bad. Keeping it was stupid though. If someone was sticking around they would be defenseless. Why not leave, check out of the Inn before anyone found the bodies. All the killer had to do was leave, the name on the register could be false and no one would know any different. No one had left, no one checked out, no men from the airfield vanished. Why would they stay? Stepping outside, there were airmen everywhere.

"Sullivan, you finding anything?" Brock called.

"No, sir."

"Tell Kingfisher I want to know everything about Petya Ivanov or Volodymyr Kompanichenko. Get back and don't stop until you can answer that question."

"Sir?"

"Unless you can tell me about him I don't want to hear questions."

"I never could figure out why he was here."

Brock turned back to him. "Why is that?"

"We don't fill the goods needed, we're an intermediate field. Gas and sometimes we add on some equipment, bombs."

"Nothing to liaise?"

"No sir."

"Do you have something to do with this harassment?" Mr. Poole growled.

"No one steals from me. I hear there are thefts and I thought it was exaggerated, now my own papers have gone missing. I don't care if you're inconvenienced. Someone in this place..."

"You cannot do this. I am citizen of the United States." Poole yelled.

"Then file a complaint. We found stolen jewelry in the office." Brock started to walk off, Petya was down by the water and he headed over. Surely something could be cleared up.

"I am guilty now because I am a Soviet?" he asked before Brock even said a word.

"If I was doing that I'd have shot you already."

Petya's shoulders relaxed. "Then what?"

"I don't suppose you received any coded messages that have gone missing?"

His blue eyes narrowed. "We are allies. Why should I have coded messages about help you are rendering my country?"

"That didn't answer my question."

"No, sir, none have gone missing because I have received none."

The odd thing was Brock couldn't tell if it was a lie. He usually could. "Any thoughts about why there were some found among Jane's papers?"

His eyes went wide. That got a surprise out of him at least. "Can I speak without being thought a spy? I am here to make sure the lend lease goods are flowing quickly. That is all."

"If it might be a reason that got her killed, I'll take it as what it is. A lead."

"She came to me about buying some information last week, but I couldn't make any sense of what she showed me. I turned her down. Told her if she wanted to get money for things like that, she needed to find someone far higher up than me, and certainly not in a place like this. The embassy might have a better chance, first of knowing if what I was shown was worth something, and two, having the ability to pay for it. But if they were dealing with her like that, it wouldn't be code. That she asked me I would say means she is an amateur, not an agent. They would have sent someone to collect it from her and pay for it. Not a coded message."

"Not you then?"

He smiled wide. "Certainly not me. The NKVD does things like that, Trotsky did not die of old age. They wouldn't have gone around and killed 4 people to get one though. They would have been far more subtle."

"Shouldn't you be far more subtle about telling me about them?"

Petya shrugged fatally. "They have put me in a gulag once already what can they do—kill me? I have no family left to threaten me with. I would rather stay out of prison here for a murder I didn't do than worry about what people thousands of miles away might do for the mere mention of their name. These murders are an amateur compared to them."

"If you could guess what would have them interested in coming here of all places?"

"There is only one thing they want, they want to know about the nuclear bombs. Everyone knows scientists were getting close before the war. Everyone was waiting to see if the Germans developed it, but with the Russians in Berlin I would think it is unlikely they will find it there. It could have saved them the war if they had it ready. Jane wouldn't have things like that hiding around here of all places, would she?"

"And yet there is far more going on here of all places than I would imagine."

"No. It is far more interesting than I thought it would be."

"And to answer your question: no, nothing like that was found." It was a partial lie. Magda might trust the man, that didn't mean he had to. They hadn't found anything, but there were hints it might be there somewhere. "I'll let you go," Brock said suddenly, then he broke into a run. Magda said Jane had bought the place from Harold's son. If he told her everything...

"What's wrong?" Charlotte called as he ran past.

"I grew up next door, the owner of this house raised me more than my own did in many cases."

"There's a hiding spot?"

"If his son told Jane all about the house she just might still use the old safe. Downstairs was gutted, but up here wasn't."

Brock found the panel in the main bedroom, and pulled it free of the surrounding wood. Kelti and Charlotte peered over his shoulder. "You know the combination to the neighbors' safe?"

"Give me a minute, it was a long time ago. The date he was forced to leave China."

"When was that?"

"When the Boxers rebelled." Brock turned the dial back and forth and back. Then he turned the knob, the door swung open smoothly. A gun sat on top, the same era as when Harold left China. For a moment he thought no one had touched it since Harold, but moving that aside, the book was a diary, Jane's diary.

Brock grabbed it all and locked it back up. "Well are you coming or sitting here?"

"Where?"

"The boat. The smartest of us all is sitting there."

"I have to come, don't I? I'm your driver." Kelti announced, grabbing his hat.

"I'll grab the check-in book. At least we'll know the sequence of events," Charlotte added.

The airmen were all lounging about the dining room by then.

"Anything?"

"No sir, we've walked the entire grounds, searched the out buildings, even the rooms and nothing."

"The rest of you that have work to do, get back to the air field. Those of you that don't, stay here, no partying, the first drink that comes out puts you in the brig. I want them watched. Someone committed 4 murders." Brock took Greg's hand as they scrambled out the door and put the gun he found in it. "Greg, stay here and make sure Mrs. Heinrichs is safe. Magda too. We can't send everyone on their way until we have some clue, so if someone tries to leave, make up something to keep them here. I'm counting on you."

Looking over, Roy stood there at the door, not saying a word until then. "Who gave you permission to look into the murders?"

"General Maxwell, I believe, as well as the airfield. Do you have a problem with that too?"

"I didn't have a problem with Dresden, I just asked a question. You seem to have a problem with questions."

"No he doesn't, that would be me. He answered you

110

rather politely, I thought," Magda said from the door as she lit a cigarette. "Do you wish to discuss it further? I'll gladly argue with you over it. I just didn't want to do so with Brock and Greg at the table. You see, I know what men at war have in their heads and it's not sitting there discussing the horrors."

"Are you saying you condone..."

Brock walked out.

vi.

The place wasn't terribly far up the road. Chuckanut Bay was barely a cluster of houses you had to turn off the main road to see from the highway.

"There you are, Brock! I was wondering when you'd come see me," Mrs. Trevelyan called, coming out of her house.

"Been a little busy, found out my wife was here and I have a son."

"Here? What do you mean here?"

"Well I don't think my father let anyone know she was staying with him. He sent word I was dead and then she showed up. We're still trying to figure out why he let her stay."

Her face lit up. "You mean that nice girl and boy that you always sailed with. You married her then, oh god that's why you were thrown out. She's half Japanese and your father would never abide that."

"We never said we were married, this was solely off the fact we said we were engaged. And that was before the war. She had to finish school. I wasn't going to stop that. I had just gotten my wings. When China came up, Harold pushed me to go, and we needed the money. I left behind a son the last time we saw each other."

"Where is she, then?"

Brock pointed out to the boat at anchor. "Harold left me his boat. We have her livable if not completely comfortable yet."

Mrs. Trevelyan peered out into the small bay. "Why don't you pull it up to my dock here, and you can come to supper."

"Sure, never turn down your cooking. Don't tell anyone we're here though, please."

"Well then, you get docked and do what you need to and I'll get dinner started."

"Oh shoot, why don't you go get the chickens from the house? Who knows what will happen to them when the fraternity gets a hold of the house?"

Mrs. Trevelyan gasped. "He didn't."

"I asked the lawyer yesterday. I was cut out completely, and something called Beta Theta gets it. They said I could go in and get personal things though."

"And you won't fight it? No, you wouldn't, would you? Not after he treated you so badly. Well you go on. I'll see you for dinner."

"Your wife is half Japanese?" Kelti said once they were alone.

"Yes, and I'll shoot you right now and let them find the bodies if there is anything brought against her."

"That's the argument you were having with your father." Kelti muttered.

"Yes, and I might have mentioned that sooner if I didn't have to defend myself against murder charges."

Brock yelled, and Amy came up on deck. He waved her into the space where Mr. Trevelyan had a fancy racing yacht tied up once. He'd gone down some 20 years ago now.

"We were invited to supper, and Kelti was assigned as my driver, so he has to come along," Brock informed her as Amy threw him the lines.

Amy turned her head to hide a smile. "Find anything out?"

"There was another body with Smitty. I'm guessing it's Emily Vaughn. They're here to find her after she escaped from prison."

Amy looked perplexed as she stepped back for them to bring aboard the boxes and salmon. "Well now we know who was hiding in Cabin 1."

"What?" Kelti cried.

"You mean she was there while we were?" Charlotte gasped.

"A woman had cabin 1 for the last three weeks now. Jane said she was her cousin. She was out and around most the time, but about a week ago she started taking her meals in her room.

We went and checked the room; it was cleaned, she was gone. She was here the day Brock came back from the dead, though."

BJ came running. "Come see my room, Dad. We were making it perfect."

"After I look, how about you take a nap in there and test it out. Mrs. Trevelyan asked us to dinner tonight and you want to stay awake for that, don't you?"

BJ pulled him in, barely giving him time to put down the box he carried. "See?"

All his toys and books were stowed and secured; a few pictures were up on his walls. Clothes put away. He had moved in.

"I wanted my special crab pot, but that's on Tom's boat."

Damn, he forgot about that. They weren't bringing things in on a rowboat; he'd forgotten all about the boat. "All right then, let's get you in bed, and I'll see you in a while, ready to visit."

BJ nodded and climbed under the covers before Brock shut the door. "Where's the boat?" he asked the moment he got out front.

"I think you've missed telling me something." Amy said quietly.

Brock sat down and told her everything he'd found out since he scared the death out of her. Not quite all of it. Petya for instance, Kelti would have a field day with that information.

"Tom's boat is the only way she would have been getting away if she hadn't already left by car, and two of them were found where they could only get if they were on a boat. They must have been getting on the boat when it happened. Smitty was taking Emily, and he'd come back to get the others or with the rest of the goods," Amy said finally.

"So back to where I asked 'where's the boat?'"

Amy nodded slowly. "But why wouldn't someone have taken it to get away, why would a murderer stay? Give a fake name, check out before the bodies were found, or even just vanish in the night. There aren't masses of people running around the country killing inn keepers."

"There has been mention of blackmailing people into getting information—it could be possible they grew disillusioned with the party with Emily in jail, if they were forced into it.

Sympathetic once and not now. If it was found out they were planning on leaving, escaping their reach," Charlotte said.

"Yes but why not leave now that it's done?" Amy asked so simply. She started running through all the papers that were sitting in the boxes.

"That's everything I found in Greenly's office. These are Jane's I found in the safe." Brock pushed over the pile. "We haven't looked through them yet."

Charlotte opened the small box among them and let out a low whistle. "Damn." She dumped out dozens of gold coins and a very nice diamond.

It was the papers that had to have something. But as they went through them all nothing caught his eye, at least.

"Brock, dear, is it all right if I kill one of those chickens you said I could have? You always love my chicken and noodles, and I really don't have enough to make for so many." Mrs. Trevelyan asked from the door.

"Yes, of course, however you can use them. Rather that, than they starve to death locked in a cage." Brock looked up slowly. "Mrs. Trevelyan, I don't suppose anyone along here has seen Father's boat?"

"Oh. He had it tied up at Eliza Island, has ever since they started looking close at boats coming south from Vancouver. I guess someone was catching on to his little arrangements, or there were many arrangements besides his to deal with. He would unload there, and bring it ashore days later in the small ketch."

"And you never turned him in?" Charlotte accused.

Mrs. Trevelyan smiled like an old devil. "Knowing something and catching it happen are two different things. I've had decades to figure out his methods, I know when conditions would be right for it, but even if I had the volunteers on the lookout we never caught them in the act. I called and had the Inn checked out and they found nothing. Man was more devious than I am, I guess."

"Awful long row to take two people out there to get away," Charlotte muttered.

"Oh no, he never would have done it the night he was killed, and he has a motor for it now. No moon at all and the storm coming in, he wouldn't have been able to see a thing, all that mist."

"He and Jane were dead on the shore, they just found Smitty and a friend of Jane's across the way at Larabee. The only way for that to happen is if they were in a boat when they were shot."

Mrs. Trevelyan let out a radiant smile. "Oh, I didn't mean he wouldn't have been out, those are the nights he brings in the goods if you can catch which misty night. I just meant he wouldn't have been leaving with the mist like it was. That was even before the storm came in."

Brock had been away too long. His father's ways and he never changed them.

"Brock, you have that look," Amy whispered.

"What we saw in the kitchen. They hid it in the pantry, just having cases sitting in the outbuildings are rather obvious. In a pantry in a restaurant it's expected. There's so much there Mrs. Heinrichs can't keep track, if they sold it would she notice it gone? Mrs. Trevelyan, you told me about it the day I got here."

"Oh yes dear, they've been selling it all over town for years. It was Tom that was the head, Jane sold it. Mrs. Heinrichs would give it out under the table though when she knew someone needed it. I never wanted her in trouble, I know she's just stuck with it all."

"She said Jane threatened her with being accused of spying if she didn't keep her mouth shut."

"Spying?" Mrs. Trevelyan murmured and sank onto a bench. "Is that what you're sitting out here figuring out?"

Kelti looked horrified that he had told her just like that.

"4 people were killed, Jane had papers she shouldn't have, and there have been thefts of papers for years, I guess. They were caught up in something."

Mrs. Trevelyan scratched her neck. "Go get the chickens, dear, while I think. There's something I know I heard, but I'm old, it will take some time."

Brock tossed the chickens in her coop and got back to the boat. She had hardly moved.

"Mrs. Trevelyan, they're in your coop."

"Thank you, dear. I remembered what it was. Jacob mentioned that there are odd telegrams going in and out of the Inn. Jane would come in and very carefully tell him something incomprehensible, make him repeat it as he sent it, and a day or two later she'd get one in return. Just as odd."

"I would have thought mail was more secure." Kelti muttered.

"Did he ever say what sort of odd?" Amy asked.

"He said it was the lyrics to that song, "We'll Meet Again." Another time it was the "White Cliffs of Dover." Always a song, the lyrics to it, not the title. His wife sings with that band, so he knows all of them."

"What if the sending is the signal, what's in it doesn't matter? There's something to pick up, for instance," Kelti said.

Brock turned to Amy instantly. "Is there someone that comes often? If she sent word that she had something to collect, and they came--but that wouldn't explain why they were killed."

"It wouldn't matter anyway, since I've been here I've never seen any of the guests more than this visit, other than Greenly. And he wouldn't have to pass anything on, he had the info at his fingers. Not to mention no need to send telegrams. He could have done this any time without killing anyone."

"Hell!" Brock growled.

Mrs. Trevelyan stood. "I'll get dinner on."

"If it's not Greenly, or any of us, then who exactly is left that we're talking about?" Kelti asked.

"Poole, Carlson, Ivanov, Magda, those are..."

Amy shook her head. "Why hasn't anyone left? One murder should have driven them away, but there have been 4 and no one leaves. Are they so miserly they prefer a room rather than getting killed? Sitting here pretending we don't know anything is harder than if we could just start asking questions, but if we choose the wrong one to start, it will spook the others," Amy muttered. "And if we just say the place is closed there's no keeping track of them."

"Why hasn't anyone left?" Charlotte repeated. "It's been days, and it's a hotel, no one's left."

"She does long-term rentals with some night-by-night. Greenly was the only one there for the weekend. It's the fact no one has said there were people dead outside my door, I have to leave—that's what gets me. We're trying to get the boat done as fast as we can to leave, and they just sit there like nothing happened. Regardless of guilt, no one's left a murder scene."

Brock cleared the table. "Forget everything that's happened since. What is true that we know for certain? When did Emily Vaughn get out of prison?"

Charlotte grabbed a piece of paper.

"About a month ago, somehow she got a doctor to claim she was deathly ill and needed surgery. She was taken out supposedly on the edge of death, and the moment their backs were turned she stood up and just walked out. We knew she had letters from Bellingham so we were sent to see if she showed up. Which, according to Mrs. Harker, she'd been here since almost as soon as she left prison," Kelti related. "Those telegrams, those ring a bell, come to think of it. Found in her cell after she left. They'd been planning it all along, her escaping."

"Sir..." Charlotte had the guest book and was running through it. "Sir. The doctor, he's in here. Dr. Simon Eberstark about 4 months ago."

Amy nodded. "I remember him, when I had just started here. He was from back east somewhere, we talked the week he was here visiting his sister. He said she had won a stay at the Inn, and since she lived there in town she thought she would treat him." Amy's hand went over her mouth, covering a look of horror. "There was a big stink here, he was found in his room with a prostitute. It had to be at a party like the other night. He swore they met here at the Inn and they got friendly, nothing more, no talk of money at all. She said she was from Seattle looking for work. Would have meant absolutely nothing except his wife was the head of the decency league back home. They held it over his head, it made a stink here, but if it didn't make a stink back where he lived..."

"That would make sense," Kelti said quietly.

Brock walked out onto the deck and hit the wall.

Amy rested her head against his back. "What's wrong?"

"What could I say if you did fall for someone else, you thought I was dead? All because of my ass of a father. I never wanted you to have to know about him."

Amy kissed him gently, stopping his venom. "That's not what's wrong. That wouldn't send you out here hitting things, that was your father and you've known about him for a long time, not anything mentioned now."

"You shouldn't have to live with a bunch of prostitutes, you shouldn't have men attacking you like you are one of them. I've heard how they treated you. I can handle leaving you, it was for far longer than planned, but I'm not the only one living with it. But I'm fighting a war to protect people when my own wife safe at home might as well be a prisoner. If we never figure this out, if I didn't know I wasn't the killer I'd arrest me right now for the thoughts in my head. Whatever my father was doing letting you stay, I just can't see that it was for good. He got you the job with Jane, Jane..."

Amy slipped her arms around him. "You are a good man, I know that. I know you hated him and don't give a damn he's dead. I know you can figure this out because you're his son and you hated him. Then we'll live the future because I love you more than you hate him."

"Fighting for a country that..."

A gentle hand caressed his cheek. "No, Brock, it's not perfect, but we could be in Japan, where even my going to school was all but impossible. We could be in Britain, where a smuggler's son could never dream of being a colonel without a title. I was all but running a department, General Maxwell had control, he just swanned about while I worked, and that had nothing to do with being Japanese, that was because I was a woman. When the war is over they'll send me back to being a secretary maybe. I never was attacked until that night, and you taught me how to keep it only a stolen kiss if it had ever happened. You always said I was the smartest person you ever met. Not woman, person. God, Brock, do you think I married you without anyone else ever showing interest? You think I stayed true to a memory because I was lacking offers? From the moment we met you showed me how to be anything I wanted. I didn't have to be a little wife, and I watched you wanting me for years, but I was your best friend's sister. There are some things I can't escape though, being a Japanese American woman is one of those. I was given a brain and it told me you were the one that would let me be more than what I was born to and I was lucky enough to be born here—that I could make the choice of a smuggler's son who was kicked out for letting me tell him I can't live without him. Even dead you're a hard act to follow, Brock. Hating the US for doing what everyone else had to do to get through this war won't change anything. Now go back inside." He barely sat down when Amy poured him a drink.

"So we know Emily arrived here a few weeks ago. Were they planning on leaving or not?" Kelti asked. It was clearly changing the subject.

"They'd have to, wouldn't they? A woman escaped from prison doesn't just sit there. I can't imagine giving up a prison cell for a hotel cell for good," Charlotte added.

Brock picked up the diary that lay there among gold dollars. It was hard not thinking about the war, going back to it especially. Orders that kept him right there, it seemed impossible after so long. The war left his mind as he stared at the pages; it wasn't a diary in the journal sense, no, it was more a record of something. Lots of initials, dates, only by comparing them with the guest register could he figure out what it meant. There were dozens of names, just about all of the ones with a rank before their name. Some system was getting them there, no one was going to just drive by the place en route to well, anywhere. It was the end of the road. "Were there many of those stays given away?"

"Yes I rather think there are. I was put to stuffing envelopes once she sent out dozens of them at a time. She said if you get the commanding officers you'll get the enlisted men. Not many showed up though compared to what was sent," Amy answered.

"She had a system going, didn't she? But why here? It's the end of the road," Charlotte murmured. They were going through everything, and everything was giving them nothing new anyway. Figuring out what she was doing after it was over seemed rather simple.

"When was it Emily was arrested?"

"Before the war, but just barely," Kelti said vaguely.

"You were in China when it happened, not long before Pearl," Amy elaborated.

"She might have bought the house, planning on settling here, when Emily was arrested suddenly and then the war started. 'Jane you're part of the movement and in place, we need information.'"

"But nothing says why her contacts would kill her out of the blue," Kelti muttered.

Brock couldn't help but laugh. "Now you know why I rather thought you'd done it, it made more sense that the US would want her out of the way than her own people. They're getting information, even if it's lost because they go to some island to start over, they aren't compromised. No one knows there's a spy here. You just have a connection to an escaped prisoner."

"I didn't know Emily was even here until Amy said she was," Kelti defended.

"That's just it though, tracking Jane doesn't seem to have anything to do with this. Unless there's something on her calendar saying Meeting with a specific name on the evening of black market delivery, there's not going to be something to figure this out, not looking through here. She might not have known they were coming even."

"We'll get out of your hair then and see if we can't think of something new when we've given it a rest," Kelti said, and they left in an instant.

Brock watched them vanish down the road, before he looked over at Amy.

"Why are you looking at me like that?" Amy whispered.

"Do you know what those calculations are for? You wouldn't know if it had anything to do with plutonium."

Amy sat down hands over her mouth. "How did you hear that?"

"Kingfisher called someone to find out what Hanford, Washington was about. I was seeing Greenly's pages in his office filled with him getting it wrong, and I heard you in my head saying one of his women was from there. Later he said as much that one came and helped him with the work a few weeks ago, the only time he said his papers were ever at the Inn. His father got him where he was so he wouldn't be sent to fight, he knew he couldn't do the work. The blatant women was him trying to get fired without saying my father bribed people to get me here. The only ones who know that one word are you, me, and Kingfisher. He says he was stationed somewhere around DC, is this farmed-out work for something like that? I have a theory but I want to hear what you think."

Amy grabbed the papers pulled from Greenly's office. Slowly she leafed through them, muttering to herself. "Nothing's together for any project. There are divisions all over the country. Aberdeen is the main place, but many universities have people working on things on campuses keeping it compartmentalized. We were kept in the dark for many things, no one trusted me with anything until I switched offices. When I was breaking codes suddenly I made it through the barrier from drone to queen bee. There are thousands that can do math, there aren't quite so many that can figure out the secret secondary code even after the transmissions went through the process when they're sitting there translating, not supposed to figure out anything." Then she looked up at him with a grin. "Is your theory they knew Greenly was an ass and pawned him off with something useless?"

"Are you more of a genius than I thought you were?"

"No, but years of little more than just math and codes, I'm a fast genius. The codes at the top show they're for North Africa, you couldn't read that in those copies that Mrs. Heinrichs found. Heat and humidity affecting ranges and such. We haven't bombed there in years. Who's his father they don't want to anger?"

Brock could only shrug. "Kingfisher knows they're brothers, but it wasn't in either file who the father is."

"I don't suppose you asked Petya about the codes?"

"Yes, I did. I didn't want Kelti hearing though. He says he's never received any codes at all, so they can't be stolen from him. He also made a comment that if it was the NKVD involved, there wouldn't be 4 bodies, they'd have killed their target without drawing so much notice as 3 extra corpses. Called the killer an amateur. As far as him just telling me lies I'd keep this in there with your other secrets, it sounds like Magda has him ready to desert, he's not even who he says he is. Some friend of Petya's that wanted out of Russia. I guess they aren't kindly to Cossacks. The real Petya was killed in the war after his papers to come here were cut. She says if she thought he was anything other than what he claims she'd deny him a new start, and that's deterrent enough to keep him in line. If he goes back playing Petya and they see what happened, he's dead."

"And you trust Magda?"

"Amy..."

"No, nothing like me making a fool of myself and thinking you were interested in her with me in the other room. I suppose I had a bit of what you must have felt when you saw that Private kissing me in the middle of the dance floor. Just do you trust her?"

Brock poured himself another drink. "Yes. She knew the Earl of Moerhab before the war, and he gave her a house on an island near Greece and Turkey. She married a prince, yes, but he was poor as dirt. The two of us had more growing up than they did, I guess. She had a son on that island, they had to slip away when the Germans came. They can't be sure, but that boat of refugees are some of the few that survived. He's living in Scotland now in a castle, the Earl of Moerhab is friends with the Duke of Cairnmuir, they all vacationed on the island where she has a house. They were all good friends before the world exploded. She wasn't in Czechoslovakia when the war started, she has been sneaking into Europe all along. The Duke has been housing her son since '43, she lives there when she's back now. Her husband's cousin flies with the Allies like her husband did before he was captured and died, and I see him rather often. He can't keep his mouth shut, probably because no matter how impossible it sounds, I wouldn't doubt the rumors."

"That means that we're running out of suspects though, if no one is lying," Amy muttered. "Brock, your instincts were always spot on."

"You want me to say who I have a gut feeling about, I've said it all along. If I trusted him I'd be saying all this in front of him instead of just you. The only person that there's a true motive is the government itself. I really don't have a clue if we're being played in something, but the feeling isn't going away. My biggest argument against being played is that if this was sanctioned there should be someone coming in and sweeping it under the rug. Not you calling a General and it lands in my lap. Intelligence wouldn't leave it to me if it was their show. Kelti's my first suspect, but if he did it there's something wrong. Petya too, I don't know what it is, but something is off."

Amy looked back out to the shore, the car was just leaving. "Hell."

CHAPTER 6

Brock woke to an empty bed, the sun was long up though. He found Amy sitting out on the deck, staring at the view. Chuckanut Island lay opposite, a little bump of land, beyond far more massive islands. Sitting down behind her, she only had a robe on in the cool morning. It fell off her shoulders easy enough, he forgot how silken her skin was until he kissed her shoulder. "What's wrong?"

"Mrs. Trevelyan knocked a while ago. It's all over the radio when she got up. Germany surrendered yesterday. It's Victory in Europe."

"Are you kidding me?"

Amy's smile was massive as she nudged him. "You think I'd joke about something like that? I thought you could use some sleep, so I didn't start screaming."

Brock pulled her back against him, but just rested his head on her shoulder.

Amaya snaked her arm around his neck and held him close. "There's time still before BJ wakes up if you want to celebrate."

He pulled her back to the berth.

ii.

Amaya lay there with her head on his chest when BJ came running in and scrambled up on the bed. At least they were covered. He nestled between them over the covers and fell back to sleep.

"I think we wore him out yesterday," Brock whispered.

"What if we can't figure how much Jane lost in secrets? How many men just stopped in and things were taken."

"You here?" Kelti called from the deck.

"Yeah we're lounging in bed though, give us a minute."

"I thought you would want to hear..."

"Mrs. Trevelyan came over earlier when she heard on the radio." Brock called.

"We were wondering if you were sailable, nothing's open today with the celebrating, I know it's a long shot, but wondered if your father's boat might have a clue."

Brock started pulling on clothes. "If you could help get the sails set up, sure. Amy moved it on the engine, and we don't have gas for that option long distance." There were some black market cans left of course, but if they kept running around as much as they were they'd be out quickly.

"Sure. We had a little boat on Lake Superior when I was growing up. I'm some help, not an ocean sailor though."

"The man that built the boat has it set up for junk rigging, one person can handle it practically, once they're strung up at least." Brock covered BJ up since he wasn't even stirring at their talk. He reached around and buttoned Amy's shirt for her. "I will have to have a normal work schedule here at some point. What sort of disciplinarian can I be if I'm breaking all the rules and nothing gets done?"

"Oh, Kingfisher runs that place, you're just there to make it official."

"I thought you never left the Inn much, and he said he wasn't welcome before you arrived."

"The maid was there when they were all partying, it wasn't Stephens they told the newcomers to go get a flight they wanted, it was Kingfisher. If they wanted something specific for meals. It was everything. I think you can have your late mornings without too much concern."

Kingfisher—he'd forgotten asking about Petya. "Good to

know, for days the country isn't celebrating." He kissed her neck. "Let me go make a call first."

Mrs. Trevelyan was out when he stepped in the house to put through the call. Finally Kingfisher picked up.

"Sir, did you hear?"

"Yes, it's the big news. I wanted to give everyone a 12-hour pass, I can't suspend flights that are scheduled though."

"Luckily we're waiting for a group to come before we have anything to do. Tomorrow."

"Then the airfield has a 12-hour pass, but I expect them to be functional tomorrow."

"Thank you sir."

"Sullivan told you what I asked, didn't he?"

"Oh yes, I was making calls yesterday. I couldn't find anything about the other one."

"Well if there was anything to find on him it would be in Russia, I think. It was a long shot. But anything about Petya?"

"He lied to us. When he arrived with his orders we gave him a room based on that. No one ever checked."

"What did he lie about?"

"Well from what I can tell there's no such thing as a lend lease liaison. He's known all the info though. Someone with the Soviets had to have told him everything."

Hell!

"Then you think he's a spy? What on earth could he find out here, of all places?"

Brock just sat there staring out the window. What was left? "He's here officially though?"

"The best I can tell is yes. I had his orders in my hands, and they looked as real as the rest I've seen. They were signed by the Russian embassy."

There it was. Spies never would have handed out papers showing government authorization. And that left? "If we think that Jane was stealing info, I suppose someone had to be buying it. If he was spying, he's not trying very hard to hide who he works for, which is stupid, and he's anything but that. A go-between? The real question is what was he buying?" Hell, the real question was how much Magda had told him about her in getting him supposedly turned. Even if she said nothing, the minute she went somewhere communist they'd know she wasn't sitting around knitting. Maybe he'd been around her enough to see the Princess slut was an act. Any photo he could get of her could be sent around. Heaven forbid he caught wind of her father going back. "Shit!"

"Sir?"

"You have your 12-hour pass. Celebrate. I'll get Petya with me to keep an eye on him."

"Should I call intelligence?"

"For what? The Soviets are allies, and we have no proof of anything. It's a guess. We'll figure out what to do tomorrow. Today we have a reason to celebrate at least for a day. Tomorrow it's back to the war."

"Yes sir."

The phone went dead, and they were in serious trouble.

iii.

They were sorting out the sails when BJ finally woke up.

"What are we doing?" he came out asking without a pause.

"We're going to go for a little sail. There's no work today, the entire country is celebrating so we're playing hooky from work."

BJ jumped up and down. "Can I help?"

"Sure, take that rope there and put it into loops. We need all the tangles out so we can rig the sails. You can wrap it around something if it will help."

"Yes, sir."

"Kelti, what did you mean by blackmailing people when you mentioned it yesterday? Do they do it often?" Jane was selling something, and it surely wasn't information from random passersby. He'd have little to sell if he came around on leave.

"I don't really know." Kelti shrugged. "It's a rumor we were told more than anything. Why?"

"Well I kind of wondered how they would do something like that here. We thought about it yesterday, but during dinner last night it just sort of kept crossing my mind. Even if they sent invitations to every officer in the country, who's to say they would have anything worth stealing on them? It's a crap shoot as far as possible results."

Kelti sat back on the railing. "You're right. Do you think they would use the setup they had to get help from the doctor on military men coming through? Get them caught having an affair, drugs, something. Then comes a letter after the fact, weeks, months later, saying we'll tell unless you do what we want. That would make far more sense really; it wouldn't matter where the Inn was located at that point. It could be in the middle of Kansas as far as that mattered as long as there's the parties—what better cover to bring in professional women or opium, or anything really."

"So where's the proof? There isn't much to blackmail unless there's proof. That's what's in your head, I take it?" Charlotte asked.

"Something like that. Nothing that really gets closer to who killed her though."

"How could I ever not have seen all this going on in the time we sat here searching for a woman?" Kelti muttered.

"If that's right, there was nothing to see, unless the right man was here, and even then most likely it would have just looked like a man taking a woman to his room." Brock stopped. "Damn, there has or had to be a camera of some sort if that's right."

"There is," Amy said behind him. "I just about got my head taken off when I opened Jane's room to clean once and Jane saw me." Amy sat down. "Hell, I never thought about it, it pointed through the wall. I could only just see it, but it was just near the wall."

"What room?" Kelti demanded. "We searched them all yesterday. I would have certainly noticed that."

"It was...I only saw it once. No idea where it could be now."

"Unless there's another hidden space?" Charlotte said, hopeful.

Brock couldn't help. "Nothing I know of, and I think if I knew the safe location and combination I'd know where they are. If there was something I don't know about, it would be downstairs where she had the remodeling done, but that's not very private to hide things." Brock couldn't help but start smiling. "What if they already bought an island property and have a place there? Jane could have been going back and forth preparing for when they broke Emily out."

"There are over 100 islands though, it could be anywhere." Kelti cursed and BJ stared at him.

"170." Brock hopped off the boat deck and ran to Mrs. Trevelyan's house. She came running when he pounded on the door.

"What on earth, dear?"

"How would you like to go on a jaunt around the islands? We're celebrating."

"I'd love to."

"Then tell us where dad sailed most often and we'll go. Did he take Jane anywhere?"

Looking up at him slowly, Mrs. Trevelyan grinned. "He's been making stops on Saltspring Island every time he does a smuggling run. I used to spend summers there a very long time ago with my cousin. I spent last summer there and saw your father. Helen said he'd been coming often, sometimes there was a local woman with him that he left and would come back for."

"You didn't say before?"

"Well, you didn't ask before, did you? If you wanted to know about Canada I'd have mentioned it, you just wanted to know where his boat was."

"I don't suppose you know if Jane owns land there."

"Oh sure, her family home is there. They got it as a pre-emption back when they still did those there. Jane didn't know I knew her father from my youth, oh that man was fun in the barn. That was back before Mr. Trevelyan came along, never quite as fun, but far better as a husband, let me tell you. That man abandoned them for years at a time and she had to scrape for every morsel. Mother died of tuberculosis when she was a tyke. Sent to live with American relations when she was 12 or so. There was talk she tried to come back home after he abused her but her father wouldn't have her. He's gone now, dead of the drink."

"Could you get us in the house?"

Mrs. Trevelyan nodded quickly. "I imagine my cousin could find us a way if it's necessary. There's a brother that still lives around there. Tell him we're looking to see who murdered her. Hopefully someone's sent word she died."

"How about we call the sheriff and ask him to make sure they know while we get the sails finished. It will be a while before we get up there, we don't need to be the one breaking the news. I don't suppose there's anything else we need to know, I don't care on what topic. Do you know if Jane sold the Inn? You seem to know everything."

The old woman just laughed. "Well my husband might not have been from around here, but my family was one of the first in these parts when there weren't roads and we could just get here by boat. Related to just about everyone. The Indians to the mayor, I can claim them all, a lot like you, but you've been gone to not hear all the talk."

Brock snorted. "My grandfather showed up in the 1890s when the gold rush north faded, we hardly have any connections other than my mother's family, yours were here in the 1850s. Do you know anything? If Mrs. Heinrichs knows, she's not saying anything that helps other than she found papers that showed Jane had secrets she shouldn't."

"I don't know about spying, dear."

"Right now we just need to know about Jane to try and find what got her killed. Someone was hiding there after escaping from prison and, we think, getting ready to start over at the home on Saltspring."

She shook her head. "Not if they were hiding, if they didn't want anyone to know, that would be the first place they'd go. She might be hiding things there since she was visiting often, but if she had something to hide." She shook her head again. "Most everyone knows she's from the area even if not from Bellingham itself. You go get finished rigging, we should still go there, maybe my cousin has heard some news, or the brother."

"Give us an hour or so to get the rigging up then. We're almost ready."

"I'll make us some egg salad sandwiches then, I suddenly have more eggs than I know what to do with."

Kelti looked up when he got back. "So?"

"Saltspring Island, she's from there I guess, there's a house, but she's not sure that would be the final destination. If they're hiding, everyone around here knows she has the connection to it, I guess. We'll go up and look for the boat around Eliza, and run up to Saltspring. You might want to grab clothes." When he turned back, Mrs. Trevelyan stood on the dock. "Yes?"

"You asked if she sold it? I didn't think about it a moment ago, but at the Monday meetings I go to Jane did as well, and her cousin came with her a couple times. When we were asking about this cousin she said she was from Gabriola Island, but now that you asked I don't think she was from there, she didn't know names mentioned, and it wasn't people."

"Then let's go," Kelti demanded.

"It's farther past Saltspring, we can do both. She might not have even wanted Tom to know where she was going, it wouldn't be hard to take a run from one to the other if she had a small boat."

"Go get clothes, we'll be gone awhile. Tell Greg and Magda to come along. Petya too. We'll make it look like we're going on a sail to celebrate. Not a spy-hunting expedition." He'd never lied as much in his life as he had since he went on leave. Or maybe it was that he'd never been lied to so much since he went on leave.

"You trust them?" Kelti snapped.

Brock shrugged, he trusted Magda more than the man asking the question. There still wasn't proof the government wasn't behind the deaths. "We can make up a story to go run to houses and such while there's sightseeing for others."

"I can do that," Mrs. Trevelyan offered. "I know all of them. My cousins had a small ketch we'd sail around when I went for visits."

"Well then we need to supply the boat, and get these sails up." If he was wrong.

iiii.

Eliza Island stood only a couple miles from the house. Even before they reached the boat, which quite clearly was anchored in a small harbor, Brock knew there was something wrong. A small little island, but it had a beach they dropped the others at to have a picnic, and Brock went for a 'walk' with Kelti. Each foot closer the signs of the boat being ripped to pieces grew clearer. Hatches were all open, sails unrolled and hanging into the water.

"I take it we found proof that they're looking for something," Kelti said quietly as the rowboat approached it.

"I think we have." Brock climbed up on the deck, and it was a disaster. Not a single cubby for storage was left intact, not just pulled clear, they'd been broken open with an axe or something like it. There were still crates of goods sitting there, opened, but contents intact. Brock started picking up what was usable. No reason to waste it.

"They were caught halfway through their delivery." Kelti murmured.

"Looks like it. Father had a small runabout with an engine, it wouldn't take as long to get out here and back a couple times. Straight east of the house you could make the run in the mist and fog with just a compass. He'd be a fool if he was out in that gale we had. He's no fool. If they were found when Tom and Jane were on shore, they were killed while Smitty took Emily out here to load up, then when the boat returns they kill the other two. They might have even forced them to show them where the boat was before they were killed and dumped overboard. The runabout is probably sunk or something, blood would make it hard to hide by just walking away. Then they just walked into their room and went to bed or even went back to the party."

"The police asked everyone their movements, everyone seems to have left for a time. Everyone came and went. Everyone had the opportunity unfortunately to get away for a few hours without notice. I suppose which is how they planned it, they could slip in and out while the party kept everyone distracted if it was noticed she was gone for too long. Who would notice the innkeeper while there were prostitutes dancing around?" Kelti said quietly as he helped pick up what was there. "They really were serious about the black-marketing business, weren't they?"

"Only thing the man ever did to make money, if it wasn't this, it was some other scam. Hardly ever worked a legitimate job and I was the one kicked out for marrying against his wishes. You sure you didn't do it?"

Kelti laughed out loud. "I'm a history/politics major, most

are detectives or investigators of some sort. I'm a researcher in the background usually, I thought here was worth checking out, and no one else did, so they said go yourself. I can tell you the history of wars and politics. But killing someone, no. I'm doing my part for the war the best way I can. Charlotte came along to get men to talk. No one seems to have known Jane was an agent at all. Until you started bringing out papers she shouldn't have we didn't know why they might have been killed. Until Emily was found I didn't know there was a connection. We were tracking an escaped prisoner."

"What did the woman do that got her in trouble?"

"Not long before the war, she was a secretary for a Senator in DC. He was on all the committees and she typed all the notes he took. One day it was discovered in a communiqué that some of those notes were making it where they shouldn't. That was before the Soviet-German pact was broken. We had some German codes broken, we couldn't find a German connection, but she had definite Soviet ties. Communist at any rate. Her parents were Russian, they came here when the revolution started. The absolute backwards thing is they were bourgeois capitalists and she saw them as a sellout for leaving in the face of Stalin. She was secretary of an offshoot group, they wanted to see America communist. The Depression was proof, they said. I don't know that she ever thought she was in danger of getting caught. They just walked in while she was at work and arrested her. Her house had all sorts of copies of papers she had taken just sitting out. Didn't even try and hide them. Probably why there's so little to find here, Jane had learned her lesson."

Brock closed his eyes as Kelti tossed a ham and some salted cod into the rowboat. "Hell, what if we're looking at this wrong? What if it's not a contact that killed them?"

"You mean someone being blackmailed? They want the proof back."

"It would be rather stupid to ignore every possibility just because we know she was involved in one thing and it might be another."

"If we find anything you want to look through it all and see if we recognize any faces from the Inn. Can't hurt anything. But for now I'm starved, how about we get back before they eat all the food?"

Amy pulled Brock down to her. He didn't care if anyone grinned at a man resting his head on his wife's lap. The sun was coming through the mist for once, and no one grinned. The view of Mount Baker was spectacular, getting away from the hills allowed it to rise as if floating in a cloud over the land. White-capped, it held dozens of feet of snow on its peaks. Of course all that only due to no clouds.

"You didn't wake up last night," Amy whispered brushing the hair from his forehead.

"Didn't I?"

"No."

Brock kissed her palm. "I must feel safe with you."

"Anything there?"

"No, but I'm guessing they were killed while they were running things to the Inn, his boat was destroyed when it was searched. Only thing that would explain where the bodies were found. The killer took the boat out to check it, probably made Smitty take them before they killed him."

"So, on to Saltspring?"

"Yes. We have nothing else to go on. This is just maddening."

"I never meant for you to have to deal with this," Amy whispered.

"It's not that, no one would have come to Mrs. Trevelyan to hear anything and this would be even farther behind. It's just the fact that we have nothing to go on, we keep finding things telling what Jane was up to, nothing about someone that would want her dead." He hadn't had a chance to be alone with her since he made the call. He was lying to his wife now too.

"What are you doing here?" someone said suddenly. Petya jumped in the air like he was ready to be shot on the spot.

They all turned to find a man there with a gun aimed at them. "Well, I'll be damned if it isn't little Brock." He lowered the gun and pushed his hat back.

"How are you, Mr. Knutson?"

"Wondering why your father left that wreck of his on my front door."

"He was killed a few days ago, we think the person that did it made the mess. You can salvage it if you want, I wasn't left anything of his and you're right, it was a wreck even before they messed it up."

"He was what? You mean someone was out here doing that to the boat while I slept right here?"

"We were at the Inn while it happened too. They were shot—the only answer is a silencer."

"Well, I'll be damned," Mr. Knutson muttered and sank on some driftwood. "Are you back for good then?"

"I was supposed to be on leave, but just was given command of the Airfield here at least for the time being. Maybe you haven't heard, the Germans surrendered yesterday, it was just announced this morning. We're taking a little sail around to celebrate."

"Hot damned. Sounds like I should come to town more. I might not have heard that for weeks." He grabbed Mrs. Trevelyan and planted a big kiss on her. Even as he sat there his feet did a little jig.

"Why, you sweet man," Mrs. Trevelyan cooed like a school girl and batted at his arm.

"Where can I get in line?" Magda teased and the man winked at her. Brock just watched as Greg pulled her over. If she was going to argue it died quickly.

"How far are you going?" Mr. Knutson asked, ignoring the kiss beside him.

"Victoria, maybe further, depends on the winds," he lied.

"You call that a little jaunt? Well I suppose after your summers around here that's not too far. Damned nice boat you have there, what's its name?"

When Greg let Magda go she looked at him with completely different eyes.

BJ beamed. "Night Rain."

Brock pulled him on to his stomach, tickling him. "Harold left it to me in his will. I guess he wanted to go on a sail around one last time and died before he could even tell me."

Mr. Knutson started smiling as he watched them. "I loved me a woman named that long ago, for a night anyway. Night rain—always loved the sound of it. Beautiful name for a beautiful boat. And beautiful women. I'm surprised he didn't just call it Amaya."

Amy started laughing. "I never thought about it, that is its meaning, isn't it? She said he wanted the three of us to come."

"Makes sense if he was leaving it to me all along."

"Colonel." Something in the way Magda said it made him stop cold. Out on the water was another boat. Just a small one, but something about it...it was Tom's runabout. He'd assumed it was sunk, obviously not.

"Mr. Knutson, do you have another gun?"

"What do you take me for, an easterner?"

"Then I need to borrow that one. Ladies get on the boat nice and slow like we're picking up to leave. Someone has my father's runabout and the last time that was seen was the night they were killed."

Only then did Mr. Knutson turn to look at the water. "Oh."

Amy picked up BJ and fought the urge to run. Magda had Mrs. Trevelyan out of sight down below like the woman needed help walking. There was no missing that she pulled a pistol out of her handbag.

"Get in the house and stay there, anyone comes and it's not us, shoot them. Don't ask questions first." Mr. Knutson walked off as Greg and Kelti went on board.

Charlotte stood there staring and Petya grabbed a hold, pushing her along.

"I can't make out who it is," she protested.

"You do that undercover."

Brock pulled the lines and set sail. They had a head start of sorts, at least. The runabout had a motor, and they were stopped cold. But pulling the lines, the sails filled with wind. The junk rigging really made it simple for even one man to handle a boat. More made it easier, but Harold had planned well to have a long-term trip. Just enough room to not get on nerves, enough storage for supplies, and an easy rigging. All he was trying to do was get away from the island to keep Knutson out of it.

"Amy, take over and make it look like we're out for a sail, just keep the speed on as much as you can." Brock ordered as he gave up the controls and positioned himself in the back. If they were paranoid the boat would turn off, if they were right...

"Charlotte, down in our room, the closet, there's another gun on the shelf, you want to go get that. They're coming after us."

Greg handed him binoculars, keeping down. "Can you make them out?"

Brock peered through the eyepieces, the face behind them wasn't one he expected. "It's Roy Carlson."

"That little idiot."

"You know anything about him? He said some rather odd things, but nothing personal."

"He was getting too close to Magda last night, she didn't like it. He kept asking her about her husband. Seemed to know more than that she liked about the real woman." A bullet slammed into the boards very near Kelti's head. "Damn." Greg pulled back from sight even further.

Another bullet hit nearby.

"Damn it." Brock stood up and took aim. He knew the man saw him; the boat turned abruptly. At the crest of a swell Brock fired. Roy looked up and the quiet unassuming man he'd barely noticed looked dangerous. Seriously dangerous. "I'd duck. I missed." Brock fell back behind the boards.

"Hang on," Amy called just before the boat took a hard turn to miss the point of the island. Several more shots slammed into the side of the boat.

"Well I suppose we can't say there's no proof for who did it any more," Charlotte snapped as she held on to the mast to keep from sliding.

"But who the hell is he? Communist agent or just pissed-off victim?" Magda asked.

"You want to ask him?" Greg suddenly stood up and let off several rounds. The boat still was in a turn and he fell, unable to right himself.

Magda rushed over to him lying there, he was grinning. "Sail around the island Amy, he should be swimming by then."

"Damned idiots." Roy yelled at them.

Brock looked over the edge, several holes were in the small boat and the engine. "Nice shots."

"Well when you want something hit you ask the artilleryman, not the flyboy. You never could hit anything when we went hunting. Colonel." He tacked that on with a grin.

Another shot sounded in the silence and they all ducked.

Brock went and took the helm after they were out of range of the disabled boat.

"Who was it?" Amy whispered.

"Roy Carlson. Greg said he was asking a lot about Magda last night."

It was all over her face, not the one she expected. "Brock, he just showed up a night or so before the murders. Emily, she'd been hiding for a week now. The first couple weeks she went around like she was on vacation, then she just stepped inside and other than delivering meals I never saw her."

"What? Finally some proof someone was lying, but who?" Amy's head shook slowly.

vi.

Running around the small island, there was no missing the remnants of the rowboat not quite sunk out of sight. No sign of Roy Carlson though. Not swimming, not on shore.

"There," Magda called.

Brock spun, Roy was floating in the water quite motionless.

"Hell," Greg muttered. "I didn't hit him, I know I didn't."

"No you didn't. He was still cursing us when we left him." They weren't far from the shore. It would have been an easy swim. "I don't think he knew how to swim." Brock pulled off his shirt and pants.

"I know you belted me for saying it before Amy, but damn, you lucked out," Charlotte muttered, and Magda turned her head, hiding a smile.

"Luck, I fought for him. You think he wanted to go behind my brother's back and sleep with his best friend's sister?" Amy answered just before Brock dove in.

The water was cold, but it wasn't far to reach the man. Something was wrong. Very wrong. The man hadn't drowned, a bullet hole severed his neck artery. Damn! They had the boat tied up by the time he reached the dock.

Petya helped pull him out, and Amy had a blanket ready. When he came back from getting his clothes on they had his wallet out.

"This says he's Roy Carlson from Iowa." Nothing else. No, he couldn't miss Amy pulling a small slip of paper from the wallet and tucking it behind her, no one else could see it.

"Is it safe?" Mr. Knutson asked from the trees nearby.

"Yes."

"I can take him in for you, I'm guessing you're not out for as much of a jaunt as you said. I was thinking of going in for the celebration when I heard the news. I can tell them he was found off the island, and his wallet wasn't on the body. You can go in when you're done and have him identified, should give you a few days."

"Sir, you take his word on it so simply?" Kelti asked.

"Oh heavens, Brock saved my life when he was but a boy, 15 years old and he came out with me to fish the waters past the islands in true ocean. Couldn't pay him hardly anything, but when we were swamped and I fell in, he jumped in and came to get me. His father would have let me drown. Go on, get out of here."

"Mrs. Trevelyan, why don't you go back with him? Take BJ too. I didn't think anyone would be shooting at us when I said you could come along. We can talk to your cousin alone as well as with you."

"Are you sure? I must admit 85 might be a little old to be running around like this."

"I'd feel better knowing you were safe."

Mrs. Trevelyan kissed his cheek. "Then you'd best get going." She took BJ's hand. "Come along. I need a big man to keep me safe while they're gone. Can you keep me safe?"

BJ puffed up his chest. "Yes."

CHAPTER 7

i.

So many islands, hills silhouetted on the horizon, and Amy lay on the deck, soaking in the infrequent sun. Math genius suited her well, she could do work in half the time it took others to program the problems in machines. Magda just smiled and lay nearby. Suddenly it seemed to be near 70 degrees.

"So Brock tells me your stories should be believed no matter how unbelievable."

Magda started laughing. "If he heard them from Vladen he probably shouldn't believe them."

"Then you didn't help catch German SS officers that were coming to England in a U-boat to play English," Brock asked.

Magda sat up quickly and turned to him. "How did you hear about that? Vladen wouldn't know of it, no one should know of it but the few of us there. Northstar's life is in danger if it gets out. You think I'm impressive, that one was inside a general's office in occupied France for years. Bloody idiot of a general sent Northstar back to another country once the hunt was off. Spent the entire war playing a German, if Vladen...I'm only saying that much because the Germans surrendered."

"I've been liaison with the British as well as flying," Brock said quietly. "I thought it was an exaggerated anecdote he told to sound impressive."

"You met the old bull, he was a bloody idiot then too. Brodie wouldn't risk Northstar. When did he tell you that?"

"When there were bombing plans being made before D-day. Told the whole room how the entire North Sea defense plans were snuck out of the continent."

"What are you two talking about?" Amy whispered.

Magda just narrowed her eyes.

Brock just smiled. "She was big in code breaking until someone called her in for who her father was. She's higher clearance than I am, I'm sure. She's no maid, that was a temporary job because the entire world is in chaos."

Magda looked around carefully. "The contact I met here, we were sitting at the castle of the Duke of Cairnmuir, debriefing me about the situation at home, he'd escaped a concentration camp. Bloody awful week, let me tell you. I'd found out my husband died just before. My son was on an island the Germans had invaded. The duke himself was sitting in a Japanese prisoner of war camp. The duke's brother was supposed to be coming home to keep the home fires burning and playing host to a friend, wanting to let a friend of his propose like the old days. Middle of all that I'm walking on the shore and I find Northstar washed up on the beach. An American model that spoke 7 languages, in French clothes. We half-swore she was an enemy spy. She'd been there 2 days before we found the fisherman that was getting her out of the Germans hunting her. There was a traitor and names got out that shouldn't have. First thing out of her mouth once we knew she was ours was she might have said something but seeing as two German SS officers were eating with us she didn't think she could trust us. She'd spent 6 months underground and every time she'd set up an extraction it went wrong. The men were there to try and get info out of the duke's brother. He worked for the old bull. Wrong place to land, we pulled off hiding my contact, hiding she'd washed up, until the Germans must have called in to say they weren't getting anything and someone heard where they were. Someone in the Bull's staff way down had told them who she was because she had checked in, ordered her to die. The man proposing was a doctor though, he saved her life. Got us a U-boat blown out of the water, letting them call to be pulled out. Not to mention a spy in Whitehall, and two Germans. She'd barely recovered when the Bull said oh, you speak Dutch, let's send you off again. Anyone calls me good, I just laugh and say I play a part for a couple weeks; she's doing it as her life. No training either, she was just an American in Paris when it fell and managed to get hired on with a new name on her own records. Best damn infiltrator I've ever met. When she ran, most thought she was a turncoat German. They were willing to track her to the ends of the earth too when they realized she had the whole North Sea defense plans going through her hands a week before."

"And your son?"

That at least made her smile. "Got word during all that he was on a boat to Cairo, he's been at the castle now since. Duke's brother got word his brother had died a year before, and word just got out. Northstar learned for the first time both her parents had died years before. Brodie would marry her in an instant, assuming he survives the push to free his brother's men, and on to Japan and if she survives her assignment. I haven't heard what happened to either of them lately. Too much chaos."

Greg stopped next to Brock as he steered them along Orcas Island, Magda stopped talking though. Sleeping with him or not, she didn't tell just anyone what she did. "Now how long will we be sailing until we get to our first stop?" Magda asked.

"It's going to be hours even with making good time. From here Matia, Sucia, Patos, after that we'll cross into Canadian waters to find Stuart, Saturna, and Pender before docking on Saltspring. 50 miles, 60 perhaps."

Brock only watched as she slipped her fingers in Greg's and pulled him toward the stairs down. "Don't worry about me, I always find something to keep from getting bored. Do you know the Chinese make books to give to brides showing them how to satisfy a husband? I found one when I was cleaning the boat. I should hate to be a boring bride."

Greg's eyes opened to a pair of blue eyes inches from his. The look in them was one Brock knew well, Amy had seduced him with that look. They'd married that very day. "You would even consider..."

She put a finger over his lips before he said "a man with one arm." She'd hinted before though. "I consider men that adore me and you, sir, adore me. I would consider if ever asked, but until I'm asked I'll just have to practice." Magda just pulled the man behind her.

"Now I didn't see that coming," Amy muttered. "Not the bedding part, but if she's a princess, well, she mentioned marriage."

"Come here, I need to talk in private," he whispered.

Amy narrowed her eyes but came over standing behind him like she was trying to get him the same place Magda had Greg. "What's wrong?"

"Magda was in your sight all the time, wasn't she?"

"You don't trust her?"

"Did you see her or didn't you?"

Amy kissed his back. "She kept trying to pull me out of the way, worried I'd get hit."

"No pistol out?"

"Yes, but she was more worried I'd get hit, she was never aiming it."

"What about Charlotte or Petya?"

"Greg had the gun you sent her to collect. Petya was down below, helping Mrs. Trevelyan. Why are you asking?"

"Carlson was shot in the neck. Greg was right, he hit the boat and the engine. I looked just after he shot and the man was moving around and pissed, he wasn't collapsing on the ground dying. I'm not sure the last shot was him shooting at us, but someone else on board shooting at him. If he was unable to move the boat and sinking, he would have been swimming for shore."

He felt her freeze against his back and she rested her head on him. Amy shook her head against his back even as he watched Kelti sitting at the front of the boat. "You're saying he didn't want anyone to talk to Carlson, which means everything he's told us is suspect. Is that finally the proof you were looking for?"

"Unfortunately."

"Then who is Roy Carlson?" she whispered.

"That's what really worries me. If we were lied to about one thing, what else is all a lie?" Brock pulled her around and sat her on the console in front of him. Amy looked up slowly. However did a woman like her fall for him? Even at 17 she was stunning, she belonged in a painting of Venus. Statues of Aphrodite. He'd seen photos of her grandmother, and she could have posed for Japanese masters, even if she was a farmer and walked around the house in a plain blue kimono. There were times she would look up over the table when he came to dinner and he could see the exquisiteness Amy inherited still visible at 70. Her mother was a good solid farmer's daughter, a good mother, but not really graceful and sublime. A Gibson girl she was not. She fell for a Japanese man, at a time no one did that sort of thing. She endured 25 years of prejudice for the man she loved. Amy talked of him teaching her how to survive, that was catching her own fish, and belting a man that wasn't a gentleman, every ounce of strength she learned from her mother. Every single ounce she learned from a woman that forgot her before the end. Until the war she'd never once hid that side of her. Amy wasn't to hide, it was just American, and she and Harry were definitely American.

"What was that paper you pulled from his wallet?"

"You saw that?" Amy slipped a hand along the top edge of her bra and the paper appeared. "It's in Russian. I don't have a clue."

"We have trouble. I've been trying to get you alone since this morning. I had Kingfisher looking into Petya since this started. Sullivan couldn't even see why he was in Bellingham of all places. A liaison would be where it was ordered, loaded. They refuel, and do a few things. There's no reason he should be there. Kingfisher said the papers he received were signed by the Soviet embassy and there's no real liaison. I'm starting to think he was here to buy info from Jane. I still think if he was a spy himself he wouldn't admit to being part of their government at all. That's why I had him come, to keep an eye on him."

"He was down below, he couldn't get a shot from there. He didn't kill Roy."

"No I think we have two to deal with. One that killed Jane and one that was to meet Jane. I just can't say if it was part of a sanctioned kill, or not. If it's not, then I don't know why. Who the hell is Roy? And if Petya isn't really one to desert, then that means Magda is in serious trouble, if he realized she's Resistance and sent word off, if her father is headed home and the Russians get there first, he's dead."

Amy chewed on her fingernail for a moment. "Brock, I think I know who Roy is. He found the note in Russian. He's government, and a hell of a lot better at it than Kelti. Those comments he made that pissed off you and Magda. What if something happened at the same time as Dresden? He was asking where you were at the time without saying it. Finding out if you were involved. Greg said he was asking about Magda's husband, she didn't run around telling anyone she was married. I didn't know anything until she came to the boat. I thought you were flirting. Someone government would be able to find out her activities. He could have been trying to find out how much she might have given away. Or pumping her for information on his target."

"Petya, you want to go the storeroom and grab a bottle of whiskey," Brock called throwing all caution to the wind. This had to end soon.

He was back in an instant, grinning. "Decadence."

"What does this say?"

His eyes narrowed as the paper was slipped over. He downed a gulp from the bottle. "Now I am suspect again?"

"Now you're translator."

"Where did you find it?"

That right there answered him. He'd seen it before. Where it came from didn't matter otherwise. "What does it say? Or I can tell someone about Petya dying."

He looked at it for a moment before his eyes closed.

"What?"

"Well, either you're in serious trouble or you're turning me in, because you obviously know what happened."

Brock could see the wheels in his head turning. Petya was running hard. "What does it say?"

"You're holding a Russian message saying they will pick up the package tomorrow, escape and payment will be provided as agreed. There are some coordinates at the bottom."

"What are those?"

Petya grabbed the charts near the wheel. With a look at the minutes on the side the frown said it all. "Well, close to here." It took him a little longer to narrow down the spot before his finger finally stopped at the top of Vancouver Island. "I'd say a submarine. Should have guessed, most would make me the first suspect and you hardly blinked."

Brock shook his head as he took the bottle. It burned its way down. He felt like shooting the man then and there.

"You did suspect me?"

"Everyone."

Petya wandered off, Brock didn't stare, but there was no missing Petya looking back at them. There was fear in his face at long last.

"Where is that letter we found from Emily?" Amy whispered.

There was only one answer to hear her ask like that. "A code?"

"Well, if no one seems to think that she truly had a woman lover, and if it was Emily in the room hiding, and no one ever noticed anything going on, there doesn't seem to be any other reason to write it. I've gone through everything we found in Greenly's office, Jane's office, all the safes and hiding spots at the house in my head and I just can't think of anything we've found that has a clue we've missed. The letter is the only thing out of the ordinary. We looked at everything else minutely."

Brock pulled it out of his pocket and handed it over. "If there's any time to be a genius now is the time."

ii.

Brock pounded on the door to the berth. "You guys done yet? I waited a couple hours."

Greg could be heard laughing. "Yeah, just talking."

"You want to help get these bullet holes covered up, I don't want to pull into port with proof we were shot at for all to see."

In an instant, Magda opened the door fully dressed. So much for lounging in bed. Brock stepped inside the small room before they could leave.

"Are we ignoring the fact that Roy was killed? I know a bullet wound when I see one." It was barely a whisper that came from Magda.

"I don't suppose you read Russian?"

Greg's eyes narrowed. "What's wrong?"

"Amy found a scrap of paper on Roy."

Magda nodded. "Sort of. I'm no scholar, but I'm half decent."

Brock handed it over and there was just silence. "That...!" she screamed suddenly.

It was all she got out before Brock pushed her against the wall, hand over her mouth, the cursing could still be heard muffled.

"What does it say?" Greg whispered.

Magda closed her eyes and took several deep breaths. Brock finally took his hand away. "You knew he was lying to me?"

"No. Not until this morning. Sullivan made a comment about how he couldn't understand why there would be someone here. The airfield doesn't plan anything. With no clue I had Kingfisher check him out even with your impression of him. This morning when I called to give them a 12-hour pass he told me there's not really a Liaison. The papers he had showing his orders to check out Bellingham all had the Soviet Embassy on them."

"You think he's a spy and I was handing him my father on a platter."

"No, I think he's here to buy information from Jane and you didn't think you'd have to watch yourself on US soil."

"What does it say?" Greg asked again.

She sneered, and he'd not want to be on the other end of a gun with that look. "Our little Magda has been ever so nice in helping me to plan for the future, you really should watch her more. If I wasn't such a loving cousin she would be getting into trouble at every turn. She spends much time telling of Kapheira, perhaps we could find a vacation house there. My uncle Toshe will be returning home soon his welcome should be grand after so long away. I'll send a package home next week, it will have more than I planned on. My host Jane has been ever so generous with new clothes to help after this terrible war. I'm just waiting for her to finish collecting them. A few days more and I'll start home. The party tomorrow night should be most enjoyable, a fitting end to my time here."

"No numbers?"

"No. Just a letter home. We have two to deal with, then."

"Yes. It seems that way. Amy had you and Charlotte in her sight the whole time. Greg and I were next to each other when the last shot sounded. You were in my sight at that point. Petya was down here, doesn't give a shot. Only one left is Kelti. But I still don't have a clue what's going on. We're starting to wonder if Roy was intelligence and trying to figure it out without making a show like Kelti. What kind of questions was he asking about your husband?"

She nodded, determined. "The kind of things you don't know, and you and I actually talk." Suddenly she started grinning. "The kind of things you'd ask if you didn't know which sister I was. If he thought I was the one sleeping with Nazis and warlords, intelligence would want to know my movements. It was personal things about Branislav, that a wife would know and not a sister-in-law. I said my father really kept it quiet that she died."

Only then did she pull a gun from her bag. A German Mauser. Definitely not a woman's gun. Brock watched her walk down the tiny hall as she hid it along the small of her back. "He'll suspect you having something, whoever killed them still thinks me a brainless slut who sleeps her way around the world." Hardly more than a whisper, then she looked over her shoulder with a grin. "It's so gratifying knowing it's true for once."

"No wedding bells then," Brock asked when they got to the deck as Greg went to find some putty and the spare paint for 5 bullet holes.

"Well I'll never break down and ask like you made Amy," she threw back at him.

"I seduced him right over there off Sucia," Amy called from the wheel. She turned back and pointed back at another island. "And married him right over there in Friday Harbor. I highly suggest it, then you know it's all your fault if it doesn't work."

Magda started laughing as she grabbed the putty. "Make sure I don't fall in." She leaned over the side without even waiting for Greg to grab hold of her belt.

"Good lord, woman." Greg rushed over to her quickly

and took hold. Brock could tell when he felt the gun. He looked back at him for just a moment.

Charlotte came running over and pried off the paint lid.

Brock took the wheel again, just watching Kelti sitting there, like nothing had happened. Petya kept looking at them, knowing they knew something.

iii.

The dock at Ganges, Saltspring Island, wasn't busy, but an old man stood there. Watching. Greg and Magda headed for a shop. She hung on Greg's arm like they were long acquaintances instead of new lovers. Then she snagged Petya's arm and dragged him along.

"See if they have anything fresh, we're celebrating and there's little enough in the larder but staples. And bacon, see if there's some for breakfast, the sun's going down, we'll have to spend the night," Amy called.

"Colonel Harker?" the man finally asked.

"Yes."

"I'm Terrence Odell. My cousin sent word you were coming. She said you could use some help unofficially."

"She explained it all?" Kelti asked, looking annoyed again.

Terrence laughed. "In a telegram, not much at all, just the Night Rain was arriving this afternoon or early tomorrow and needed special help. I'm guessing the uniforms have something to do that."

"You haven't been waiting here that long, have you?"

He looked like an old fisherman really, white hair and bushy beard. "Not at all, I have the shop right there. So what help is it you need?"

"Inside perhaps."

"Yes of course." Very shortly they were upstairs over the shop. "Now then."

"Well it's a bit of a long story, but a few days ago there were 4 people killed at the Inn very near your cousin's house. We're here trying to find out what got them killed. Mrs. Trevelyan said you had told her of Jane Briggs coming here with my father. We can't find out why they were killed, we're hoping something might be here."

Terrence poured them all a cup of tea. "Well, then, someone's been telling you tales. The Old Briggs place burned down a year ago, I think it was."

"Your cousin told us, maybe she forgot about the fire. But Jane came here?"

"Oh yes, she was here, but nothing's hidden at the house."

"Would her brother know anything?"

"He was in the house when it burned. Too drunk as usual to save his own skin." Terrence sat down in a chair. "Now let me see, you need to find Jane."

"Find no, she was one of the victims, along with a woman named Emily Vaughn, my father, and the Inn handyman. They were smuggling in black-market goods, we know that much, and we have a guess about how they were running things, but if they were doing what we think, there has to be a stash somewhere. We think it's blackmail proofs. There might be nothing at all which is why we didn't go official channels. Your cousin said the other woman mentioned Gabriola Island—that's our next stop if there is nothing here."

Terrence shook his head. "No."

"Nothing at all?"

He smiled. "Oh I meant no, it's not Gabriola. Jane bought a property over on Thetis—goodness must have been 25 years ago or so. They've built an inn there, closed right now though."

"So Jane didn't stay here when she was dropped off?" Kelti asked.

"No, never. She had little contact with her family, brother and father were drunks. She did come once or twice long ago, but lately no. She'd get supplies, and then Carl would take her over to Thetis."

"How far is that one?" Charlotte asked.

"Next island up, it's half the distance of Gabriola. Maybe an hour at the most in a slow boat. Give me a minute, I can go get the keys from Carl. He's caretaker while they're gone. If they're dead, he wouldn't mind a look around. The kids were all drafted or signed up. It's been empty for a couple years other than Jane's visits."

"There's no rush, we wouldn't go until morning."

Terrence just waved the argument aside and headed down

again.

Brock sat there silent. Jane wanted it kept quiet for certain.

"What were they up to?" Charlotte muttered.

"They didn't seem to want anyone to know where they were, that's for sure, lying even to strangers that might answer questions. But why? If she was from the area, even if they gave the wrong island name, getting close would be all it would take. If you came asking for Jane Briggs and you asked for her, if Carl and Terrence knew, then most of the island knew. Why not go farther, Mexico, the Caribbean, Buenos Aires, I mean truly hiding isn't an hour away from home where everyone knows you. Go start a new inn so close to another. It's so illogical. There's something about this area, there has to be. They would be getting supplies here or Nanaimo, where I'm sure they would know her too."

"The break is Bellingham, they didn't care about anyone here knowing, but there are all sorts of blinds to keep anyone there telling," Amy answered.

"That's possible, that's the US, this is Canada. If they had a past there they'd want it kept quiet. But what the hell got them killed," Kelti muttered.

The stairs behind them creaked; it wasn't Terrence. But it was a face he knew. Curly blond hair and all.

"I didn't believe him when he said it was Brock. But here you are." Carl grabbed him in a hug. "Him and me were making runs when he was just a babe."

"There's more than one Carl around. He never said it was the one I knew," Brock answered as Carl held him at arm's length and just looked at him.

"What's this Colonel business? The radio said the Germans surrendered, are you out of a job then?"

"Can you help or not?" Kelti snapped.

"Get out. You don't treat my friends like that." Brock ordered. "Now."

Kelti glared at him, but finally walked out.

"What's going on?" Carl asked under his breath.

"That depends on whether you know anything about what the hell my father was doing. How much you don't want to get thrown in jail for their scams."

Carl snarled, "Why? What's happened?"

"Things that shouldn't be sitting around have been stolen. Dad was running black-market goods, I don't know how much he was involved in the rest. Something got him and three others killed."

"Wait, your father's dead?"

"Terrence didn't tell you?"

"I hadn't gotten to that," came his answer. "The minute he heard you were here he came running."

"I can't say what happened. We're trying to figure out why Father, Jane Briggs, Emily Vaughn, and Smitty were killed. We're fairly certain they were bringing goods from his boat to the Inn. But what was going on, we haven't a clue."

"Is that boat outside yours?"

"Yeah."

"Well why don't you get what you need, and you can take us over to my place and we can catch up. Your bastard of a father threatened me enough to keep my trap shut. I imagine I can tell you what you need."

"Nothing important when that fellow I kicked out is around. We think he's trouble, but we want to figure this out first."

Carl nodded and opened the door. "Just a sail around the peninsula, then we'll see if we can't find us some clams. I got the finest clamming bed on the island when I picked a spot."

"Then you provide the clams and we'll provide the booze. We found 5 cases in dad's house when he died."

"The old bastard he said he was out when it was my anniversary last month, couldn't spare a bottle, he said."

"What do you think you're doing?" Kelti snapped as they came down stairs.

"Well we've been invited to moor off Carl's house here till morning. We'd get there in the pitch dark as it is now. And I rather doubt Thetis has electricity to flip on like it's Times Square. And as for kicking you out get some manners before you end up in the motor pool permanently."

Charlotte came running. "You'll never guess, sir, they have halibut. They'll let us have it, no rations, because it will just go bad not used today. Is it too early do you think to make a dress for after the war? They had some lovely fabric for sale."

"How about just a dress for after work, no waiting that way. Get what you found and meet us at the boat, we've been invited to a clam dig since we have to spend the night. You might want to change out of that uniform."

She just beamed. "Yes, sir."

iiii.

Clams, halibut, Scotch and vegetables. Carl's wife declared it more festive than their wedding anniversary. Then finally one by one the others started heading to bed.

Carl's head lowered after Kelti finally left. Only he and Amy remained. "You don't know, do you? You'd be angrier otherwise."

"Know what?"

"Jane and Tom, hell, they've been together for decades, that's why your mother sent him off to France. She found out Jane had a child by him. Has a whole other family now, some 5 of them."

Brock slumped back in the chair. "You're serious?"

"I only found out about it after your mother died, we'd stopped making runs, that was years after the last time I saw you. He stood there introducing me to Jane like it was nothing."

"And did Jane know he was such a good customer at the brothels they gave me freebies because he threw me in a room and said, there's your birthday present?"

Carl rubbed his face hard. "Doubt it, she was over on Thetis with the kids. Your dad made about half as many runs for alcohol as he said, that's why it was you and me most the time. He'd fly up there in his plane, while we'd do the normal route and make him money."

"Is there a connection to Beta Theta Inc? He left the house to them."

Carl nodded faintly, but he wouldn't look at him.

"Damn it, just spit it out. I knew the man was a bastard already. He threw me out for getting engaged and then told her I was dead. That was without knowing we were married."

"Jane didn't like you existed. With your mother gone she wanted it all. Her life, her kids, her husband. Beta Theta is her and her kids, they made it legal to hide who it was. Beta the second life, family whatever it meant, Theta for Thetis. She just wanted you out of her life. You were the last thing that stood between her and everything. A couple years ago Tom came with the paper showing you reaching 50 missions, he was rather proud and she just went off saying you were nothing, it was their kids that mattered. Only time I ever saw her like that was when you were mentioned."

"That makes even less sense. If Jane hated the thought of me so much, why was Amy working there, living at the house? If Tom and Jane were together, then she knew who Amy was. If he didn't want any of us around he'd have told her she wasn't welcome when she showed up. They were letting her stay at the house, Jane gave her a job. She's half Japanese and..."

"Hell, no wonder he was acting so angry lately."

"Exactly. I never told her how bigoted he was, that's why we'd sail around the islands all summer, so he could never get at her and her brother. So why didn't he throw her out?"

Carl leaned near his ear. "I can't tell you that one, but the house wasn't left to him; your grandfather left it to you, and he was hiding that fact. Yes, HIS estate went to them, but the house isn't part of it."

Brock pulled back quickly. "And is Mr. Meter one of the kids?"

"No. Why?"

"Because he told me I inherited nothing."

"Your grandfather was his own lawyer, he didn't need to have someone do it. When your father wrote his will all he had to do was imply the house was his to his lawyer and word his will vaguely. All I own is left to... If you never found out you inherited it you wouldn't fight for it, would you? You were off at college, he bragged about how he got you back to school after the funeral without the will being read. Told the lawyer he'd let you know, big test you couldn't miss."

"You never told me. You're spilling your guts easily enough now!"

Carl put his head down. "He never let this out until '39 when you joined the Air Force. The bastard came and said he had a job for me. Next thing I knew when I didn't really want to get involved he said he'd turn me in for all sorts of crimes. For god's sake. Brock, I ran some liquor true enough, but he was talking about treason even. That wasn't what he wanted to turn me in for, that was what he wanted help with. He didn't want me anywhere near Bellingham either."

"Were they actually spying?" Brock asked, trying not to lose it.

Carl shook her head violently. "Not like what you think, she was an opportunist, she'd do anything if she could get money for it. I heard mention that they would sell things on to whoever would pay them. Their kids are involved even, getting men to come around so their parents could blackmail them or steal anything they had."

"Is there one local? I heard mention of a man that got them here like that."

"Sure, Ned Thomson. He's at a naval base in Seattle, there's a daughter in the WACs, I think they realized how much info was out there, they all came over the border and enlisted. Didn't think Canada was important enough. Why do you think her and your father got along so well—they were both con artists. Jane learned to turn her hand at anything when her father abandoned them, and she met a man just as ruthless as she was. If they got secrets from a foreigner they'd sell it to the US, if it was something from here they'd sell it to the enemy. Sometimes it was just pure blackmail to not tell a wife."

"Oh, hell," Brock said finally as the full horror of what was going on came to him. "What if Dad knew the authorities were looking at them? Somebody calls up and says their papers were stolen. Amy shows up saying she had to hide because she was being sought, you're the bloody scapegoat. When the noose got too tight either they frame you, or as a last resort they hop on the boat over here, leave you and Mrs. Heinrichs holding the bag. They've been setting you up for it since you arrived. Carl. Do you know where they would hide things?" Brock asked.

His grin was massive. "Who do you think built it for them? They never did a lick of real work."

CHAPTER 8

The weather stayed fine, considering the time of year; they woke to a gorgeous day. It was still breezy though; they made good time. Kelti was inside getting coffee when Amy stepped next to Brock and handed over the letter.

"Did you get anything?"

"Read it. It took me a little while to run through all the options," she whispered.

She took the controls and Brock stepped aside. In a small hand he could see where she had crossed things out leaving only a second message. "Please help me, my husband has framed me and now I'm in jail for his crimes. I can't stand it any longer. I know I've always told you Tom is a crook through and through, but now a crook might be the only one that can help me. Even the old trick he used to have you send him letters to hide the affair from his wife I've had to resort to implore you. Tim will kill me if I ever get out, and I'll be hung if I don't get out. He'll be the one hung for treason if I can ever prove it. Please Jane. help."

"Charlotte, what's your boss's first name?" Brock asked. She was lounging not far away.

"His name is Tim Kelti."

"Damn," Brock muttered under his breath. Finally there was proof it wasn't a government-sanctioned killing and even why.

156

She just kept going. "He's a researcher, he's not an agent. He said when he got me from the driving pool it was specifically because I had been a... He knew someone there was blackmailing Emily, if we could draw them out we could find her. He knew a connection no one else did. He officially had permission to come on what they thought was a wild goose chase." Suddenly she looked up. "She died with them! No one was blackmailing her." Charlotte sat there staring at them in shock. Her boss was a murderer.

"Go to the north edge, you'll see a clearing, can't miss it," Carl called as they drew close. Trees covered most of it, dark green as far as he could see, and then a clearing. A large house overlooked the water with a wide lawn ending at a dock.

"What on earth is that? There's hardly anyone on the island and they expect...That's what the money from smuggling built, I take it. While I was keeping us fed on almost nothing and fish and crab he was building this place."

"Well, he couldn't very well suddenly announce Jane was his wife and those kids were his in Bellingham, could he? His fine upstanding lawyer for a father, and everyone loves you. You have a good heart regardless of knowing all the secrets of smuggling. You knew the difference between doing it to survive and being a criminal. They could try and steal the house there and leave it to the kids. The Inn I imagine is left to them too. They were nasty people. I was just glad that neighbor gave you work and started treating you like a human being and not a pawn. Your mother wouldn't give him a divorce, so he did everything he could to make her life hell. Don't think your mother was a shrinking violet, she gave as good as she got. I'd take you out just to spare you hearing it. Your grandfather left you the house and the money for school because he saw the two of them being just nasty to each other. Didn't think they deserved it, I suppose. I think he knew maybe not the extent of it, but he knew Tom was a right bastard. Just skip him all together, and your father was furious. I don't think your grandfather knew what that would bring about."

Brock tied up the boat, and Kelti rushed off. Petya stood there glaring. Hell!

"Carl, you ever heard of an Emily Vaughn?"

The man shook his head. "No, but 20 years ago there was

a woman that came to visit Jane here. They walked around like sisters. What was her name, Emmeline, that's it! I think she was an old friend who Jane knew from America when she went to live with her goat of an uncle. She was going to get married after she went back, a history student I think it was. Never heard her last name."

Greg took Magda's arm; she clung to him looking properly glowing.

"Do I dare ask?" Amy asked. It was to stop everyone thinking about the fact they were walking into a murderer's sight.

Magda looked to make sure Charlotte wasn't close enough to hear. Carl was with her. She wasn't spreading her identity around, there were some she trusted, and Charlotte wasn't one of them. "He's going home with me. They will need help when the government rebuilds."

"Really?"

"She asked very nicely," Greg murmured, and Brock swore the man was blushing.

"I'm sure she did," Amy grinned.

"She is friends with a British earl that has an island in the Mediterranean; it was devastated in the war. She thought you might want to come and dock your boat for a while and help rebuild it. When the Germans left Greece they pretty much killed the whole island, and those that survived all fled, including her son."

Brock just shook his head. "And how do you go from rebuilding Czechoslovakia to a Greek island?"

"It's not Greek, he owns the whole thing. Its own private country. He gave me a house there when I married. He knew we had nothing. There were a number of Russian nobles there that fled Stalin, his wife's family mostly. They're dead now. There will be work to be done at home, but if the Soviets take over it's rather hopeless. I have a house there to repair what the war has done to it. There is no place for a princess without land or the prince that deserves the title. I'd always planned on living there. There was hardly a few months between married and war that we honeymooned there and little else."

"And the fact she presented it naked, did that have anything to do with it?" Brock muttered.

Magda kissed Greg's shoulder, just as a shot broke the silence. Greg was pulling Magda into the trees and off the lawn in an instant.

While they all scrambled to cover he could hear the cursing as a bald eagle flew away from the commotion. Kelti was no shot from a distance, it seemed. Sneaking up in the dark at close range, who could miss, but 6 people in broad daylight from a distance, now there were no pretenses. He'd given himself away.

"Crap!" Magda hissed. At least he assumed it was something like that, the sentiment in Czech didn't sound any better.

"Sir, you know something, don't you?" Charlotte whispered.

Brock handed her the letter. Just silence, and the gasp.

"I'm guessing Emily sent word that she needed help, and Jane worked on getting her out, you want to wager they were blackmailing Tim. Maybe she didn't even know. When she escaped he tracked her down. Smitty was the only one that truly was an innocent bystander. As innocent as you could be smuggling black-market goods. After they came with the first load he must have been bringing Emily out to the boat or an Eliza Island cabin until they could get her here. Probably wasn't the original plan, but then I don't think they thought Kelti would show up. The boat was probably off getting goods, when he arrived they had to wait for it to come back, so she hid."

"You knew this all along?" Charlotte hissed.

"No. Amy just finished that code on the boat since we left. We've been trying to figure out how not to get people killed, so we just pretended nothing was going on other than Petya over there letting him know we know what he was doing here."

Petya stood there confused. "He killed them." Another shot slammed into a tree near his head and he finally ducked. "I thought it was Roy. He was the one Jane said to watch out for. He was..."

"Can he get in the house?" Brock called to Carl.

"No! When they're not here they have it closed up. Windows shuttered and all that. But there are plenty of spots to take cover and pick us off."

Brock scrambled in the trees, and came around to

Charlotte. She was cowering behind a fallen tree, looking scared to death. "Who is he?"

"What?"

"You're the one that has known him longest."

She shook her head. "He picked me out of the drivers' pool only a couple days before we got here."

"And everything he told us is what you know about the case?"

"The file he showed me was what I heard."

"That Emily Vaughn had communist parents from Russia and she escaped from prison. She was a secretary to a senator."

It took a while, but her head shook again. "No, her parents weren't Russian. Her mother was a member of the Daughters of the American Revolution, and the Colonial Dames. Her father was German, came a long time ago. His ancestors served in the Revolutionary War too."

"His parents are Russian. He was speaking to me in Russian before this started," Petya whispered.

"Sure, now you're helping," Magda growled and her hidden gun was suddenly at his head. "I saw that bloody letter selling out me and my father. There's no lend lease liaison. You're buying secrets and selling mine."

"You read Russian?" He said it so stupidly. If he was a spy, he really was bad at it.

"Then you aren't as good as your letter made out," Magda grinned.

"You wouldn't shoot me," Petya muttered.

"Wouldn't I? I was with ÚVOD and the Three Kings resistance groups until they assassinated Reinhard Heydrich and brought the revenge of the Germans. If you think I'm my sister offering a decadent escape from the world, you got the wrong one. I should be watched, but not for spreading decadence among the communists, I should be imprisoned. But you aren't going to send me there."

Brock looked around the trees; faintly he could see someone moving toward the house. He was an idiot. He wasn't thinking at this like his father, and the moment he did there was a problem. "Damn it. Carl, there's a plane here, isn't there?"

"Of course there is, your father... Oh it's usually in the narrow bay north of here."

"Seeing as I'm just a flyboy, you have any ideas, Greg?"

"I do, but you won't like it." Amy put her mouth near his ear and whispered something that made his blood run cold. He hadn't thought she had it in her, if Magda had said it, maybe. It was worthy of a commando unit's determination.

"Give me a head start to get over there, I'll disable the engine to the plane then and come back flanking him on the other side." Brock grabbed the gun out of Magda's hand and shot into the air over the house before giving it back. He ran out onto the open lawn, fast, hoping Kelti was too busy ducking to see him. He just made it to cover when another shot hit the dirt behind him.

Turning back, he signaled to Magda. There was no missing her shoving the gun at Petya's head. "You're the distraction, walk up to the house or I'll shoot," Magda snarled.

"You wouldn't dare."

"He can shoot you or I can, and I'm a better shot. With him you have a chance." She shoved one last time, and Petya stumbled out onto the lawn.

The pine trees were thick, but Brock just darted around them. He'd never once stepped foot on the island, but he'd sailed around it, anchored in its coves. A long narrow channel lay on the north edge next to a cove, it would be a tricky landing in the plane, just the sort of thing his father would revel in. The man could have been a great flyer, but no, he had to become a criminal. A shot in the silence made him stop suddenly. Looking back, Petya lay there, still writhing around. In that instant though, Brock looked around. Hell, he'd been on the island. They picked up liquor loads right there, the house hadn't been built then, but his father...shit, his father was having him play with his brothers and sisters. He'd go and talk to the supplier, leaving Brock to play. The supplier he never saw. It was probably Jane. That was long before Prohibition and the war though. What on earth, supplier of what though was the question? Or was that all a story to keep his mother in the dark about another family?

Brock kept running even while his head was reeling, so many things when he was growing up had meaning now. The fights his parents had. His grandfather had fine standing in town, well thought of and admired. No wonder he knew little about all of this, the man was damned ashamed of it getting out, even to family. Keeping it to his father being a known smuggler was enough of a job. His poor mother knowing though. She'd have been the laughing stock if it was found out. Bad enough she was married to a man like that, he'd thought Father did it to anger her, now it seemed more that he didn't care. Doing what the hell he wanted without any thought to anyone. He could have left, but no, sitting there with another family a couple hours from her and his own father, he was just being nasty. Hoping for a house and estate if he stuck around. Grandfather knew though. He knew his son was a bastard. He left him nothing, and Tom stole it.

The Curtiss plane appeared on the water through the trees. What scheming, scamming, blackmailing, black-market business had they been up to? Not to mention the Inn, how had they paid for so much? Even stolen when he was passed over, his grandfather had nothing like that. A thousand dollars given to fund college in cartography, mixing his talent for drawing and knowing the land like he did. That was all there was. He'd looked for a job in that, and nothing came of it. The Air Force was second choice, and the 45 a month was lucky. With the Depression easing but not still ended, there wasn't much other choice.

"That's far enough, Colonel."

Brock turned slowly before he even touched the plane. Kelti had a pistol aimed at his back, even though he stood some 20 feet away.

"You think I'm stupid."

"Magda was shocking us that she's talked Greg into going to Czechoslovakia with her to help rebuild."

Kelti raised the gun aiming it at Brock's head. He was a very poor shot if he missed at that range. "Don't joke with me. The Russians just freed Prague, she's the biggest anticommunist I've ever met. You don't seem very surprised I'm holding a gun on you."

Brock just stood there completely unaffected, to tell the truth. "I should have been dead a long time ago. Maybe if you asked me 4 years ago I might have been surprised. Maybe if you had done it before I found out my father had his other family here with 5 kids, a house the size of the likes I can't imagine how he paid for it, oh and he was trying to steal a house left to me because no one told me it was mine. Now I have to figure out why you're shooting at me. I've got more on my mind, frankly."

Kelti ran at him, shoving the gun right in his chest. He truly did look like Hitler screaming at a rally, red-faced and fanatical. "Do you think..."

Brock brought his hand up and closed it around Kelti's hand and the gun, slowly with effort he lifted it, aiming it at his own head. "Then do it!"

"I know you're here on leave for fatigue, is that what they call going crazy?" Kelti's attention was lessened in shock, Brock could feel his arm slacken.

In an instant Brock pulled his arm, the gun was aimed into space and he put all his weight behind his fist. The crack as it hit Kelti's jaw was loud in the silence. He hit the ground hard. "You obviously never played chicken with flak coming off a thousand German guns." Brock wrenched the gun from his hand with a sickening crunch before he hit him one more time for good measure. Kelti finally stopped struggling with a gun aimed at his head.

"You framed your own wife."

He looked up slowly. "I knew you knew."

"Not until you killed that man yesterday. He wasn't a threat, but he still died. Must not have wanted us to talk to him and if you didn't want us to do that, then what other lies had you told?"

"How'd you know about my wife?"

"A steamy letter we found, it was coded asking Jane for help from her husband that framed her. Amy's one of the best code breakers in the country."

Kelti sneered. "I never had to frame her, the government was just that dim. Her office, her work. Her crime. They didn't know she was so damned horrible at her job she brought her work home, I just had to copy it."

"For who?"

"Brock!" Greg called.

In that moment Kelti scrambled up and another gun appeared in his hand. Brock tried to lift his hand, but Kelti had it trapped. Just as Kelti's own hand neared Brock's stomach ready to kill, a gunshot sounded. Brock froze waiting for the pain, then he felt nothing. Suddenly Kelti fell with finality as blood trickled down his temple.

Looking up it wasn't Greg, Magda was just lowering her pistol. They were still in the trees. Slowly she walked over, Greg watching her, shocked. "Did I mention daddy taught me to shoot when I was a babe in arms? Gave me the pistol to carry the moment we went to China. Killed my first man who was trying to drag me off when I was 12. I never expected to be a princess."

"No." Greg whispered. "I got that much before today."

Brock had to say it. "He made a comment that the Soviets liberated Prague."

Magda froze. The same word he'd heard earlier broke the silence. "Petya's dead. I have to get somewhere and send word to my father he can't go back. They'll be looking for him."

"Carl, take me to this stash of theirs. I'm not turning over a bunch of secrets that have nothing to do with the war. Now."

"Yes, sir." It didn't matter that Brock was half his age. Carl wasn't going to mess with the man. He just waved him along to follow. Walking through the trees, Carl didn't say anything, silence but for the birds. The ones that weren't scared off by people running through. The house just made him sick really, he worked for hardly a dollar a week to feed his grandfather and parents while his father was building a mansion, it seemed. Wood paneling covered much of the house, and even worse, he recognized much of what had been in Harold's house. Gutting it to make the Inn, its goods seemed to have been moved there to decorate their hideaway. Brock grabbed a Chinese painting that he knew was an antique that Harold had brought back. For all the grandness, it had no running water though, a pump sat in the kitchen, and an outhouse was out back.

Carl opened a door hidden behind a wood panel in the master bedroom. A room of some 5 foot square revealed itself. Liquor of all sorts was stored there. More gold and cash, and a file cabinet.

"Go start a fire," he told Carl as he opened the first drawer. It was ridiculous as he flipped through file after file. It was a good thing his father was killed, he would have been hung if they were ever caught. Hung, drawn and quartered. Only looking through them did he see just how they built a house, bought an inn and a plane. With the amount of work it must have taken, why they didn't just get a job was a mystery. Most of them seemed to be people without access to anything military, then a name jumped out at him and then more. They were family members of people at facilities like aircraft builders, ship builders. Many that had never stayed at the Inn. Most of those that stayed there were from the Seattle area. They sent free stays to people there, people that could come on a bus.

"Where are the kids?" Brock called.

"All over."

"But they're all stateside?"

Carl stuck his head around the door. "Yes."

"They're all as nasty as dad, I take it?"

"They like money."

"Get out, Carl."

"Why?"

"I'm burning the damn house down and give me the names of the kids and where. They need to be arrested. This is Canada though, they haven't done anything here, it's all getting international authorities involved. Drag the bodies up here, throw them in downstairs." The bastards were sitting there because it was another country. They sent it all there, it would be an absolute pain to officially involve the Canadian government to get permission to search it, assuming anyone ever made the connection. They sat hundreds or thousands of miles away, hearing gossip about wives cheating on men serving, black marketing, anything they could find. They seemed to turn those secrets into information, one file he opened seemed to have gathered the entire schematics of fighter planes, bombers. Not by stealing the plans as a whole, but one daughter seemed to have collected it by making the entire plant her slaves. One person gave the nose cone, another a gun mount. More worrying, they had seemed to piece together enough bits to have a file labeled nuclear bomb. Hanford seemed to be mentioned more than once. An entire other cabinet held photos and film cans. Running through them, poor soldiers wanting a night of pleasure before heading to the Pacific were photographed and cross referenced to find the married ones.

Only one thin file had who they sold to. Hardly anything was to private individuals, it was for bigger things. Secrets they could sell to governments with far more money. He was family to... Brock grabbed several crates of alcohol and smashed them in the middle of the hidden room. Carl grabbed the money and gold and was gone before Brock took several bottles and threw them at the fire and into the hidden room, dousing the papers. He held enough to get the kids arrested for treason and who it was sold to as he watched to make sure the flames caught. The curtains were catching as he went downstairs.

It had taken longer than he thought to go through their records; two bodies lay there and the others looked grim. Smoke started to fill the air already as he walked out.

Charlotte stared down at Kelti's body. "Now what? I don't know how to announce that my boss was the traitor and killed 6 people."

"Carl, Greg, you think you can get the boat back to Bellingham for me?" Brock asked.

"Sure."

"I'm going to take the plane, Amy and Magda back, we have to get some people arrested before they can run. She has to save her father. Can you make me a list? And I don't want to hear any talk of them being my half brothers and sisters, so I should let them go."

"I wasn't going to say it," Carl muttered.

"Get out of here before there's an international incident. Get into American waters as soon as you can. We'll get this sent to the higher-ups and they can deal with the mess."

ii.

Brock woke with a scream as he fell endlessly through space without a world to crash into.

"Shhh," Amy whispered as they slept in the quarters at the airfield. The Inn was closed down when they made a call. The boat wasn't back yet, and no one really felt welcome at the house. She lay where his head rested on her chest, the sound of life in his ear and sleep came quickly again.

There wasn't much else to do. The minute Brock talked on the phone, it was out of their hands. Completely. Nothing at all left. Someone from Seattle came and collected it all, putting it on a plane that instant. Roy Carlson it turned out was a true Intelligence agent, the ones that went out to investigate, not research. When Kelti had taken off on his mission to get his wife, Roy had seen something wrong with the request. He had arrived without Kelti knowing who he was, not until that morning, it seemed. That was why he had arrived asking about sailing around, it wasn't to find anything, it was to get away. If Thetis had been bigger where there were ways to get off easily, he could have just slipped away never to be seen again. Roy wasn't catching up on the case though, he was there knowing everything. They'd been catching up and not expecting just about everyone to lie to them. All the stupid questions were just to find out if he was involved. There had been messages intercepted about the time of Dresden. He didn't want to know about the bombing there, he wanted to know where Brock was. They got that guess right.

"Mom, is Dad all right?" BJ whispered, peering from a cot nearby.

"The war keeps him from sleeping well. We have to help him get all right. Go back to bed. You need your sleep too, my little man."

"Okay," he murmured, rubbing his eyes, and fell back asleep.

iii.

"Ma'am."

Amy looked up to find Kingfisher coming in as she got coffee. Brock and BJ still slept. "Morning."

"I saw his file, about why he came back. It's hard to miss."
"And?"

"Nothing ma'am. He's not getting his leave, is he?"

"A couple weeks not dying doesn't make it go away. My brother's letters, I could always tell when it was getting to him."

"Yes, Greg mentioned him, didn't he?" He leaned near

her ear. "If you wanted to mention to the colonel, that Captain Stephens' father will not be happy about his boys being shipped off. He'll want to watch his back."

"And who is that? It would help if he knew a name."

"Senator Essex."

"And his sons both have different names? Not to mention they're from Hawaii, and there aren't senators there."

"His wife was the heiress in Hawaii. He's from Pennsylvania, they met while she was at Radcliffe. They lived there, but when she died he came back here and used family money to get elected to the Senate. They were both illegitimate sons, Stephens before he married, Greenly after. He was pushing Hawaii politics so no one had to know the connection between them. He wouldn't lose Pennsylvania, and they would gain Hawaii."

"How do you know all this?" Amy straightened up, Essex—she knew the name. It was on the list that they had turned over. She had a very bad feeling that no one would ever see that list. They'd find out that Tim Kelti killed 6 people because he was a traitor and his scapegoat had escaped prison. No one would ever hear about a house being burnt down and blackmailing rings around the country all from a family that saw profit in a war. That was why it was all taken from them as soon as anyone could get to them, nothing left behind. "Get me a call to General Maxwell, Arlington, Virginia, Cypress 1490, now."

"Ma'am."

"Get me a call through."

"If she asked, Kingfisher, I expect you to do as she asks," Brock said behind them.

Kingfisher ran off.

"What's wrong?" Brock whispered.

"Do you know who took everything last night? Kingfisher just said that Stephens' father is Senator Essex. His name was on that list you sent. I have a bad feeling that things went missing between here and there."

Brock slipped his arms around her and rested his chin on her shoulder. "That would make sense. I would have thought someone would have noticed something going on long before. Papers go missing and no one ever announced it. All he'd have to do is put their name on a list saying they were informants and when it was reported it stops them in their tracks."

"Your call, ma'am," Kingfisher said quietly in the other room.

Amy picked up the phone. "Do you have the papers?"

"Well, hello to you too."

"Do you have them?"

"Yes they were waiting here for me when I got in. The children were all picked up."

"There's a list there of everyone they sold to, is Senator Essex on there?"

She could hear the shuffling of papers. And shuffling. "No there's no list of who was sold to. There are plans and such, enough to have 5 Thomsons locked up and the key thrown away if not hung, but no list."

Amy's eyes closed.

"You're saying there's nothing to prove it now?" Maxwell asked.

"Brock and I saw it, but no not a shred of proof. You told us to hand over everything to the person that showed up. The senator has you over a barrel. I'd hope you don't need him to vote for anything related to you if he got into the papers, I'm guessing he knows you're the one that drafted his son and sent the other to Greenland."

The phone hung up without a word more.

"I'm going to suggest that once the war is over we get out of here," Amy muttered.

"That could still be years of him being able to make life hell."

"Too bad you burned proof of what he did to get blackmailed. At least you could keep him at bay."

Brock just chuckled. "They found out that Stephens and Greenly were here through his bribery and pressure. Nothing more. Not the thing you want to have get out in the middle of a war when all of your voters' sons and husbands are being sent to die while you keep yours safe from even a splinter. It didn't say their names, until you said he was the father I couldn't put it together, it just said for getting his sons out of serving. It's possible the crates Stephens was trying to hide from me were things not for him, but to pay off Jane. He seemed seriously angry at the new assignment, Greenly said he'd screwed up trying to get fired knowing he couldn't do the work his father pushed him into. He rather wanted to get drafted; at least they would teach him what to do. Stephens is of the age he might have enlisted before there was a war, and once he was in and they expected him to fight he went 'Daddy, help.'"

"Now what?"

"Keep your head down until the war is over however long that is. Then we'll sail the world, I think. Mrs. Heinrichs needs some place she can watch the house and we'll figure it out over drinks in some exotic port."

EPILOGUE

1948

Night Rain lay at anchor in Bali after sailing all over the Pacific. After the war ended, Brock was sent for a few months to arrange flights into Europe to help survivors; Kingfisher went with him. He alone got to watch Magda and Greg get married at the castle of her friend that kept her son safe. It was 1947 before they set sail. The San Juan Islands to start, then down the coast, over to Hawaii and the whole of the Pacific before finding Southeast Asia. Islands fought over for nothing more than possession of an airfield. They never stopped at them longer than supplies, they weren't ghouls on a tour of death. Just escaping the past. A soft knock sounded as Brock was teaching BJ to read.

"Yes." A brown face of one of the local boys appeared over the railing.

"Sir, for you." He pulled out a tube with a tight stopper. From it he pulled a letter before he dove back into the water.

Smiling Brock unrolled the piece of paper. The smile faded. "It started."

"What?"

"The communists just officially took over Czechoslovakia. Magda, Greg, her father, and a couple others got out of Prague, but they're not safe there."

"What, they just sent word to tell us?"

"No they're sort of asking to be rescued."

Amy turned toward him slowly. "And just how are the two of us going to rescue them against the whole of the Soviet Army?"

"Nothing like that, they were in Switzerland, I guess Petya wasn't able to send his report after all. They're asking if we want to meet them on Kapheira. There were some people that survived there, about half of a battalion that was fighting with the British, some in a boat that escaped saving her son, and 4 dozen or so on the island hiding on the mountain. They've talked to the owner about getting it rebuilt. She thought if they could buy a passenger seaplane, I could run an airline connecting the island. A bank is necessary and she thinks you're perfect for that."

"Sounds like she's making plans to take over."

Brock just grinned. "It says here she's expecting. Her contact said the money could go there to rebuild instead of helping the communists. The owner has some money from the Marshall Plan and some donations. You can sit around commiserating together. I rather think even three more people are needed even for a while just to make even a self-sufficient island, let alone a full-fledged country."

Amy stood up, well on the way to another child. "I don't know an Aegean island, I suppose we could settle for a while at least. Might be nice to have a garden and place for a baby to crawl around."

About the Author

As a Peace Corps volunteer in Kenya a few years back I traveled quite a bit and now I just wish I was. A lot of the places I've written about I've been to, a lot of them I haven't. Rafting on the Nile in Uganda, living in a Montana ghost town, Puerto Rican beaches, African safaris, Mayan ruins, European youth hostels, the Black Hills of South Dakota all fill my scrapbooks. Now a daughter takes up most of those pages, but I still travel in my head every time I write. I currently live in the Pacific Northwest and look forward to filling many more pages.

www.ingramcontent.com/pod-product-compliance
Lightning Source LLC
Chambersburg PA
CBHW032009170626
46807CB00006B/2725